What Have You Done

Also by Maureen Mendelowitz and published by Ginninderra Press
The Rock
Alone not lonely

Maureen Mendelowitz

What have you done

What have you done
ISBN 978 1 76041 818 2
Copyright © Maureen Mendelowitz 2019
Cover image: *Art in Glass* by Taryn Tollman
Cover design: Robyn Zeller

First published 2019 by
GINNINDERRA PRESS
PO Box 3461 Port Adelaide 5015
www.ginninderrapress.com.au

Do you think there's life after death?
I don't know…
But if there is, and you go first, will you wait for me?
Of course I will.
And while I'm waiting, I'll build you a castle…

For Julian. Always.

In a place of mansions, the mansion stood behind a high wall with massive wrought-iron gates decorated with smiling suns whose undulating spokes had, over the years, turned moss-green.

From a circular driveway, a flight of stairs to the ironwood door decorated with brass hinges and a massive brass knocker. Urns overflowing with white waxed blooms perfectly placed on the wide terrace.

Framed by cypresses, slim and black, and a high and wide plane tree, its leaves shimmering with starlight, the house, glowing in the warmth of chandeliers, perfectly proportioned with tall windows and a pitched slate roof.

From the garden, the smell of newly cut grass mingled with the scent of jasmine, the heady perfume of honeysuckle and the sweet scent of roses.

They walked towards the house. Towards the light.

Music pulsated down the driveway, out of the gates and into the streets – a drumbeat, the call of a clarinet, the tinkering of a piano – inviting, enticing, pulsating – tantalising the young people, making them laugh in excited anticipation.

They flowed into the entrance hall, under the burgundy light of a crystal chandelier that warmed their faces, warmed their smiles.

It was in that whirl of skirts, swirl of smoke, dusty twirl of rosy light, between the heads and moving shoulders, that he first saw her.

Her face. The curve of her smile. The sliding shadow of her cheekbones, her hair caught in auburn lights. The movement of her lips.

Her smile.

Someone stepped in front of him. For a moment, he lost sight of her. He moved forward, his eyes searching through the crowd, urgently seeking her.

She came into sight again. He stood riveted. Stunning, he thought. She's really stunning.

He did not feel Carla take his hand.

She smiled up at him. 'Steve,' she said, moving her body along his arm.

'Steve? Sweetheart?' She laughed, trying to follow his gaze. 'What is it? Who've you seen?'

He tore his eyes from the girl who was golden under that light. 'What?' he asked, not hearing her.

'Who've you seen?' she asked again, attempting to follow his line of vision. 'Who are you looking at?'

'No one,' he answered.

But she knew that he'd been distracted. She was sensitive to all his moods, was able to read his change of expression. She even thought that she could read his mind – the man whose hand she held.

Carla was small in stature. She'd long learned that, to be noticed, she needed to be obvious. To use her dark and sparkling eyes, lower her lids, flutter her thick eyelashes. To smile slowly, swing her hips, show the cleft between her rounded breasts and let her skirts ride above her knees. To have her high-heeled shoe drop from her heel while swinging her foot.

She was called a show-off, but she never cared. Men found her appealing. Cute. Sexy. They thought that Steve was lucky. He was the man she wanted. She clung to him, wound her arms around him, moved her hips under his hands, shiningly smiled into his eyes, and covered his face with a thousand butterfly kisses. She wanted to be irresistible to him, to want her as she wanted him. She'd worked very hard at enchanting him and believed that she had succeeded.

'*Nu?*' his father asked, expecting what they all expected.

'When I'm ready,' Steve said.

'How long does it take you to be ready? You've been going together a long time. What are you waiting for? She's a lovely girl from a lovely family. Her father asked me only the other day. He said, "Hymie, what's going on with Steve? When's he going to pop the question?" I said, "Leave it to Steve. He'll do it. He'll do it." To tell the truth, I didn't know what to tell him… We're all waiting. We're waiting. Her parents are waiting. Most important, she's waiting.'

'Who?' Steve asked distractedly.

'Carla. Don't you think she's waiting?'

'Waiting for what?' Steve smiled.

'Steve, stop playing games. Doesn't Carla wonder when the hell you're going to propose?'

Carla. What did she think? How did she answer when they asked, 'When's the big day?'

She was confident. They'd been together for almost two years. He would propose. Of that she was sure. 'Soon,' she'd reply with her shining smile. Her brilliant smile.

Her diamond smile.

Laura glowed as she moved to the music, her lustrous hair gleaming with russet lights, her blue dress sliding silkily her along her body.

Dancing with Carla, Steve adroitly guided her through the crowded floor, closer to Laura. He could not take his eyes from her, and she, conscious of his gaze, looked at him. Briefly they smiled. She flushed warmly and laughed. Through them ran an electric surge of elation, a recognition that something irresistible had occurred between them.

A roll of the drums.

'And now we call Steve to propose the toast to the Man of the Moment – our boy – NIGEL!'

Cheers. Whistles. Calls. A clap of hands. A chorus of 'NI-GEL NI-GEL NI-GEL.'

'Hi, everyone. And welcome to Nigel's twenty-first. Where is he? Hey, my *boet*! Come up here. Come and stand next to me.'

They were alike, unmistakably brothers, self-assured and confident, tall and athletic, with candid blue eyes and disarming smiles.

'Well,' Steve continued, 'here we all are. At my brother's coming of age. All the years my little brother. I was eight when he popped onto the scene. I'd had eight years of everything to myself when, suddenly, there was this new arrival, this bawling red-faced baby, and I was faced with a life forever changed.

'To me, Nigel was always little. He became a cute little kid whom I quite liked. I didn't even mind when he hung around me and my gang. They liked him too.

'Then he celebrated his barmitzvah and I remember smiling to myself when the rabbi said, "Today you are a man." A man? I thought. He's just a kid.

'Even when he turned sixteen and, I hate to admit, became half an inch taller than me, to me he was still my little brother. But today seeing you standing here, Nige, I have to finally admit, you are no longer my little brother. You are now my brother and you are definitely now a man!'

Loud whistles. Applause from the crowd.

'Not only are you a man,' Steve paused. 'You are a fine man. A man we are all very proud of.'

More shouts of approval.

'Especially Mom, Dad and me. Because. Not only are you a bright, intelligent guy. You are kind, empathetic, sensitive and understanding. You are also determined, focused and driven to be the best at what you do. All wonderful qualities for the makings of a brilliant doctor, and none of us here doubt that one day that is what you will be. At the top of the tree in whatever specialisation you choose.'

Loud agreement from the crowd.

'And,' Steve placed his hand on Nigel's shoulder, 'he's not bad-looking either. Hey, girls! What do you think?'

Laughter and giggles.

A girl called out, 'Definitely!'

'So. Happy birthday, my *boet*! Happy twenty-first! A long, happy and healthy life to you. Much success and fulfilment. And of course, here, tonight, amongst all your friends, all celebrating your twenty-first birthday!'

'Hear, hear!' from the crowd.

'Everyone. Let's raise a glass to NIGEL!'

'*Le'chaim! Le'chaim!*'

> Happy birthday to you…
> Why was he born so beautiful, why was he born at all…
> For he's a jolly good fellow, and so say all of us…

'Hey, Nige! Your turn! We're not letting you off the hook! Speech! Speech!'

Nigel smiled into the crowd. 'OK. OK. Look, guys. As you know, I'm not into making speeches. So this will be short. Firstly, I'd like to thank my folks. Mom and Dad. You've been amazing. Truly amazing. You've always been there for me. Supported me every step of the way. I can't thank you enough for all that you've done for me. Thank you for every-thing.'

Applause.

'Steve, thanks for all the good things you said about me. I know that I got on your nerves when I was a kid, but you were always there for me, looking out for me. Helping me. Advising me. You've been a very good brother. When you're old, I promise to look after you…'

Loud laughter.

'And now to my friends. Thank you all for coming this evening. It's wonderful to be with you. It means so much to me to have you sharing this day with me.'

Throughout the evening, between the moving figures, the tantalising slip of silky blue. A slim white arm. A graceful hand. The glint of auburn in the rosy light.

'Hey, Nige. I haven't had a chance to spend any time with you. Let's have a drink.'

They walked through the crowd to the bar on the terrace. The evening was gentle, the stars brilliant.

'It's a great party.'

'Amazing. It'll stay with me forever.'

'Nice crowd. Really nice people. I realised tonight that there a lot people here I've never met. I thought I knew all your friends, but, shows you, I don't…'

'Well, you know, Steve, how it is, you make friends in different environments. Quite a lot of them have never been to the house before… Friends from 'varsity. From the football club.'

'*Ja.* I know. Nice girls here as well.'

'*Ja.* Very nice girls.'

'Tell me, Nige, who's the one in blue? The one with the reddish hair?'

'The one in blue? I'm not too good with colours. Sometimes I get blue mixed up with green…'

'I mean that girl over there. Standing next to Phil. That one.'

'Oh. Her. That's Laura. Laura Franks…'

'Laura Franks. Is she a friend of yours?'

'Sort of. I've known her for a while.'

'Nice-looking girl. Is she linked with anyone?'

'She was. With a guy from my class. They broke up a few months ago. But why all the questions?

'How old is she? Laura?'

'Nineteen. Maybe twenty… No. I don't think she's twenty yet…'

'What does she do?'

'Jeez, Steve. You're really into her.' Nigel watched his brother's face. 'I mean, why would you even ask? You're linked. Seriously linked.' He paused. 'Aren't you?'

'What does she do?'

'She's just completed her BA.'

'I'd like to meet her.'

'But Steve, what about Carla?'

Steve did not answer. He looked across the room to where Laura was. Nigel followed his gaze.

'Did I hear my name?' Carla linked her arms through the arms of both brothers. She smiled up at Steve, pressing the side of her insinuating body against his.

'You did,' grinned Nigel. 'I said to Steve, "Where's Carla?" and, lo and behold, you appeared. Like magic.'

Carla laughed. 'Nice speeches, guys. Very nice speeches.'

'Thanks. For me, this is a very special night. And,' he smiled down at her, 'on this special night I would like to have a dance with you… that is, if Steve doesn't mind.'

The brothers met each other's gaze.

'Sure. Absolutely. Go ahead.' Steve grinned back.

He waited for them to melt into the warm meld of pulsating bodies, then moved purposefully across the room to where Laura was.

She was taller than he thought, and slimmer. He looked into the bloom of her face and saw that her eyes were topaz and her lips were softly moist.

'I'm Steve,' he said quickly. 'Nigel's brother.'

'I know.' Her mellow voice flowed towards him. 'And I'm Laura. Laura Franks.'

'I know.'

'How did you know?'

'I asked. I needed to know who you were from the moment you walked through the door.'

Laura smiled. They looked into each other's eyes.

'I'd like to get to know you. Would it be OK if I phoned you?'

The looks they exchanged were intense.

'Yes.' Her voice was soft and warm.

'What's your phone number? Just tell me. I'll remember it. I'm a numbers man.'

They were straining towards each other with their smiles and the caress of their voices. They wanted to reach out, to touch.

He found Carla's hand in his, leading him away.

'Who's that girl?' Her voice was tight.

'She's a friend. Of Nigel's.' His voice was unconvincingly casual. 'Come.' Edgily, he led her through the crowd. 'Let's dance.'

In the smouldering crowd, in the hypnotic beat of music, in the misty swirling dimness there was the mingling of perfumes, the intoxication of perspiration from damp shirts.

There was the dancing…the dancing…the dancing… Hot beat or slow and sensual.

There was a stirring of the senses, the warmth of desire, the communication of young heated bodies.

But Steve seemed detached. Removed. Carla was uneasy. Something was wrong. It was that girl, whoever she is.

Bladdy cheek! She's made a play for him. She needs to know. Right now.

Nobody messes with Steve and me… Nobody.

She found her way to Laura. 'Hi,' she smiled pertly, her chin high, her eyes glittering.

'Hi.' Laura smiled.

'Nice party.'

'Yes. Lovely.'

'So. Are you a friend of Nigel's?'

'Yes. In a way. I used to go out with a friend of his.'

'Oh. So are you here with anyone special?'

'No. Not really.'

'I saw you speaking to Steve, Nigel's brother?'

'Yes. He seems a nice guy.'

'He is. He's my boyfriend. We've been going steady for a couple of years.'

Carefully they watched each other's faces.

'In fact, we're about to announce our engagement.' Carla's smile remained but her dark eyes became sharply commanding.

Laura met her fixed gaze. Quietly she replied, 'Well, that's very nice for both of you.'

'It is,' Carla came back quickly. There was an edge to her voice. 'We're very much in love with each other and we're very happy together.'

Warily, they watched each other. Laura was silent. Her smile faded.

'Well. I'd better get back to Steve.' Carla laughed a pretty laugh. 'He'll be wondering where I am.' She turned her back and walked away with her small shoulders squared and a slightly exaggerated sway of her hips.

Laura stood quite still. For a few moments, she did not hear the music, did not see the crowd. She felt upset.

But why? she asked herself. Why was she disappointed? After all, she hardly knew him. They'd only spoken for a few moments. She wondered why he'd come across to speak to her? Why he said he wanted to contact her?

She thought that she should not have given him her phone number. It probably didn't matter, because she was now sure that he would not phone.

She danced with someone, talked and smiled, but for her the party had lost its magic. She found her friend and asked whether he would mind if they left.

'Sure,' he said. 'Whenever you're ready…'

They slipped quietly away.

Down the driveway, past the statue of a nude boy holding a flute to his lips, through the gates of smiling suns, whilst all around them moonbeams danced on silvered leaves.

She thought she'd dreamt about him. She woke thinking of him. His intense blue eyes, his smile, the breadth of his shoulders.

'Laura. This is Steve…Nigel's brother… From last night…

Oh God! she thought. It's him!

'I said I'd phone you. Remember?'

'I do remember.' In her pyjamas, she stood barefoot on the wooden floor, a flood of warmth rushing through her.

'I thought if you were available we could see each other this evening, perhaps go out for a bite to eat.' His casual words could not hide his need to be with her.

The previous evening came flooding back. Steve – Carla, Steve and Carla.

'I won't be able to do that.' Her words were rushed.

'Why not?' He waited for her response. 'Are you busy?' he asked cautiously.

'No.' She sat down cross-legged in a limpid square of weak sunlight, her hair falling forward. 'I can't see you.'

'Why not?' Steve was wary.

She waited before she answered, breathing deeply. 'You have a girlfriend, Steve.'

'Who told you that?'

'Your girlfriend. She told me that you've been together for a long time. That you're very much in love with each other. That you're getting engaged soon.'

'When did she tell you?' Groaning inwardly, he leaned back in his chair, the muscles in his face tight.

'Last night… At the party…'

'Is that why you left? I was looking for you. They said you'd gone…'

There was silence. Then, 'I can't see you, Steve.'

He heard a break in her voice.

'Laura. Please. Listen to me.' His voice was intense. 'Yes, I have been taking Carla out. And, yes, it's been for a while. But we're not engaged. And,' he added urgently, 'after last night, I know that I definitely will not be getting engaged to her.'

In a low tone, as though to himself, he muttered, 'I don't know what happened to me when I met you. You swept me off my feet. I'm completely bowled over by you.'

Her thoughts rushed through her mind. Oh God… I feel the same. What do I do? What do I tell him?

Pushing her hand through her hair, she remembered Carla – her intense eyes, the intensity of her voice. She'd declared that they were in love. That they were getting engaged. But Steve's saying no, they aren't…

Confused and uneasy, she said quietly, 'I'm sorry. I really can't see you. Not after what she said.'

Jeez. Carla. Steve thought desperately. 'Laura. Listen to me. I won't take no for an answer.' His voice was urgent and deliberate. 'Something's happened between us. And I know you felt it too. You did. Didn't you?'

Her eyes welled. She willed herself not to cry. He sensed her upset over the line.

'Listen, Laura. Please. Listen to what I'm saying. I could never marry Carla. Not after last night. Not after seeing you, speaking to you.' Then, with conviction, his words rushed on. 'I'm going to tell her. I'm going to tell her that we will not be getting engaged. That it's over between us.'

Laura was filled with dread. She did not want to hear what he was telling her.

Her answer was resolute, her voice firm. 'I don't want you to do that. I don't want to be the reason for your break-up. I don't want to come between you.'

'You won't be.' He had to convince her. She had to listen to what he was telling her. 'I haven't got engaged because I haven't been sure. If I was sure, it would have happened already. I don't mess around. I know what I want. And I now know that I definitely don't want to marry Carla. Irrespective of what happens in the future.' His voice was firm. 'The way I feel after meeting you makes me absolutely sure that she's not the person for me.'

'Well, that's up to you.' Laura did not want to hear more. 'In any case, I can't see you.' Her words rushed on. 'I'm going on holiday.'

'On holiday?' He sounded disappointed. 'When do you get back?'

'At the end of January.'

'Whew. Long holiday. Nearly four weeks. Well...' He was emphatic. 'By the time you get back, my relationship with Carla will over. I can promise you that. I have to see you again. I have to...' Again he sounded urgent.

'Steve.' She brushed her hair from her face, trying to contain her distress. 'I've told you how I feel. I really must go now.'

'OK. But don't write me off...Laura?'

'I really have to go...'

'Don't forget about me,' he'd told her. 'I'll be here. And I'll be waiting for you.'

Steve gazed at the receiver in its cradle and expelled a silent whistle, his hands folded behind his head. Staring ahead, his blue eyes slit, he leaned back in the leather armchair, with one knee bent against the desk, recalling Laura's words.

In his clinical way, he knew what he needed to do. He also realised how difficult it was going to be. Carla was in love with him. She could not be blamed for what she believed – that he wanted her, that he would marry her.

He thought that Laura's reaction was to be expected after Carla's conversation with her.

He, too, was not to blame. The attraction he felt for Laura from the first moment he saw her was overwhelming.

He breathed deeply and watched pale light filter from a bruised and swollen sky. There was a sharp crackle of lightning, a distant rumble of thunder. From somewhere came the whine of the dogs. They crept under tables when there was a storm, shivering and whimpering.

The library seemed grey and gloomy. Walls of books loomed. Steve pushed the chair away from the desk, stood up, stretched and yawned.

In the kitchen, Bella's round comforting presence was at the stove. She'd been their nanny. She was now the cook. He was her Stevie, he was now Master Stevie. She offered him oats, placing the steaming bowl on the table. He played with the porridge, letting it fall in thick blobs. Watched the blobs lose their shape.

'How's the coffee, Bell?'

'Why you don' eat firs'?'

'Not hungry. Just give me coffee. Where is everyone?' he asked the back of her.

'Sleep. They still sleep. 'Cept Ma'am. She up. But she still in bed. She have her tea. She read the papers. Why you up so early, Mas' Stevie?'

Sipping the bitter black liquid, he wandered through the house.

Boxes of unopened liquors and those packed with empty bottles were stacked in the entrance hall. Trestle tables lay sideways against the wall. Only some of the furniture had been replaced. The house was unsettled.

He glanced at where he and Laura had spoken. For a moment, he sensed her presence, saw her eyes. They'd only exchanged a few words but he could hear her voice echoing in his mind.

'Mas' Stevie? Miss Carla on a phone. She wan' speak to you.'

'Carla?'

'Yes'm.'

'Tell her I'm going into a shower. I'll give her a call later.'

'OK, Mas' Stevie.' Bella watched him climb the stairs. 'Something funny,' she wondered to herself as she bustled back to the kitchen. 'Something worry him.'

Steve took his togs and went to the gym. He did a circuit without realising it.

He dropped into his usual café for coffee and a bagel. Tried to read the newspaper, then tossed it aside.

He sat in his car outside his house and stared at huge raindrops running down the pane, trying to collect his thoughts.

He'd have to tell her. Today. He blew air out through his mouth. How was he going to do it? What would he say? His thoughts ran randomly –

This was going to cause a huge *gevult*.

She'll be devastated.

And her parents? They'll be beside themselves! God! Best friends with his! What will they have to say?

Never mind his folks… They'll go crazy!

They'll all go crazy. Her family, all her aunts, they'll be fuming.

Everybody had been waiting for it. They were expecting it. The announcement. Two years. Everyone on edge.

Now he was going to tell Carla 'No'.

There would be no engagement. No ring.

No wedding.

This was going to be disastrous. There's gonna be a huge backlash. They may blame Laura.

Carla will tell them, 'It was that girl he saw at the party. She gave him the eye. She encouraged him.'

She was capable of that. She could be malicious, especially where he was concerned. The trouble was that she was so much in love with him. Long before he noticed her, she'd wanted him. She told her friends that he was the one, the only guy for her, the guy she wanted to be with forever.

This is gonna be hard for her. Hard for her family.

Hard for his.

The rain beat down on the car. The windows bleared and fogged with his breath. He ran his fingers through his hair.

But there was no way out. He knew that. He had to break with Carla. He had to clear the way for Laura.

By three o'clock, the storm had cleared. A bright sun shone from a washed sky. Steve drove through the gleaming steaming streets, squinting against the light. He parked outside Carla's house and sat for a while again trying to collect his thoughts. What to say. How to say it.

He took his car keys and walked up the wide driveway.

The sun struck at the terracotta roof tiles of the house and light was caught in the wrought iron on the balconies. The house was Spanish, designed in respectful homage to Carla's father's ancestors, who'd fled the Spanish Inquisition in the late fifteenth century, as he constantly reminded his children. But it did have an Italian loggia, and an artist from Greece had been commissioned to paint flower murals on the walls.

'A bit of a mishmash,' his wife fondly admitted. 'But that's what he wanted.'

Chappie came to greet him, his plumed tail wagging, his purple tongue hanging in the sultry heat. He heard the sound of voices, of laughter. They were there, in the garden. Her parents, her brother-in-law, the baby, the aunts and uncles, shielded from the sun by a pagoda of crimson bougainvillea.

They waved and called, 'There's Steve.'

'Hi, Steve.'

'Carla, Steve's here.'

With a sinking heart, he greeted them, kissing the women's cheeks, shaking the hands of the men. He sensed their warmth, their approval, these kind people with their good intentions.

'Heard it was a great party last night,' Carla's father grinned. 'Carla said it was really great.'

'*Ja*. It was.' Steve's smile was forced.

'Here, Steve, Aunty Bertha's cheesecake…' Carla's mother smiled down at him. 'Your favourite.' She patted his shoulder affectionately.

'Thanks.'

Aunty Bertha's round face creased with pleasure. They were watching him, smiling at him, indulging him.

He swallowed his disappointment. He'd hoped see Carla on her own. Just the two of them. No chance of that now.

'The baby's grown,' he said, wanting to divert their focus. 'He looks bigger.'

Their gazes swivelled from him to the child.

'He is,' his granny cooed. 'He's growing beautifully. Loves his food. Don't you, little Jonty? He's gorgeous. Aren't you gorgeous, little darling?'

The aunts smiled and nodded in agreement.

From the court came the pinging of the tennis ball as it skimmed over the net. Carla moved swiftly, slamming returns to her sister, who returned them with equal ferocity. Renee, he noted, had gained weight.

'Big battle going on,' smiled Renee's husband, dangling their baby. 'Wimbledon's got nothing on them.'

Steve smiled back weakly. His eyes hurt and his head ached. He passed his hand over his forehead and leaned forward in his chair.

'Bit of a hangover, Stevie?' laughed Carla's father. 'Looks like you've got a hangover.'

Again they were watching him.

'No, I'm OK.' Steve took some of the cheesecake onto his fork.

Uncle Sam was telling them about stocks, how they'd gone up. Aunty Dora said he only talked about the ones that went up. Never told her about those that went down.

Uncle Mike was disappointed in his new car.

Aunty Hettie said, 'He likes to speed. Hates it whenever there's a car in front of him. Needs to be the first car on the road. Ahead of everyone else.'

Aunty Sarah lit a cigarette, her lipstick seeping into the creases around her mouth. She smoked and ate at the same time.

They all seemed to be speaking, saying things over each other, laughing, eating. Their voices were a jumble.

A fine film of sweat covered his forehead. A fly buzzed around his face.

He heard Carla's mother say, 'He shouldn't have a dummy. He'll get so used to it he won't want to give it up.'

Carla's father, 'Rubbish. Of course he'll give it up. Ever seen a groom standing under a *chuppah*, a canopy, with a dummy in his mouth?'

Again laughter. At the mention of the word 'groom', Steve again sensed their attention.

Overcome with a feeling of intense irritation, he stood up, stretched, and tried to smile. 'I think I'll push along. Probably need to catch up on my sleep.'

'Why don't you wait, Steve?' they urged. 'The game's nearly over. Carla won't be long.'

'Carla! Steve's leaving…'

'Carla! Carla? Steve's leaving. Wait for a moment, Steve. Carla's coming.'

But Steve was already moving swiftly down the path, leaving their puzzled looks and shrugs behind. As he turned on the engine of the car, he saw Carla running down the driveway, her face flushed, her racquet in her hand.

'Steve.' Her face was close to his. 'Hi, darl. Where are you going? The game's finished. I won!' she laughed, her small teeth sparkling.

He glanced at her then stared ahead.

'What is it, Steve? What's wrong?' Her dark eyes were focused. 'I phoned you twice this morning. You never phoned back. What's going on?'

He turned to her. His face was set, his gaze direct. 'We need to talk,' he said curtly. 'Tonight. I'll see you tonight.'

His hands gripped the wheel. He turned the key, released the hand break and revved the engine loudly.

As the car jerked forward and sped swiftly down the street, her reflection disappeared from his rear-view mirror.

Carla was only momentarily disconcerted. She'd seen Steve angry before, his face like granite, his eyes slit. She liked that aspect of him. Strong. Tough. Determined. He was good at fighting battles. Inevitably he won. That was her Steve. A winner in every way.

We're alike, she mused, languishing in her bath. We want our way. She admired her pretty feet, turned her shapely ankle. But this time he's angry with me.

She thought she knew why. He'd been distracted at last night's party and she'd made it clear that she was not impressed. She wanted his full attention. He was probably brooding about that now. He did not like being challenged. Steve needed to know that he was in charge. He was the boss of his life, the boss of his business, and he needed to be the boss of their relationship.

Well, OK, if that's what he wants. But, she smiled to herself, I will rule the roost in my own way. He won't even realise it.

Carla believed she knew how to be in charge. She was brought up indulged, a spoilt and petulant child who refused to smile unless she got her way. They all thought this was cute, and gave into her every wish simply to see her pretty little face wreathed in smiles.

Now that she was grown-up, about to become engaged, she employed other wiles to force her will.

One of her biggest challenges had been Steve, to get him to notice her, to take her out, to become involved with her. She acknowledged that getting him to commit was not proving easy, but, she felt, he was almost there. She'd even contemplated sleeping with him, going the whole way, which was frowned upon in decent circles. A girl need to be a virgin on her wedding night. But if that's what it was going to take for him to propose, then that's what she was prepared to do.

She raised her leg and studied its shape. She raised her arms and looked at them. She examined her breasts that were full and firm, and felt her flat stomach. Ran her hands over her hips. She was satisfied. Pleased with herself. She lay back in the warm water, breathing in the scent of bath oil that would enhance her smooth skin, surrounded by bottles of moisturisers and jars of creams that would be lavishly used to make her even more ravishing.

She scrutinised her naked body in front of the mirror, and smiled at her image. Tonight she would change Steve's mood. Dispel his anger. She would flirt with him, make him smile, make him laugh. Drink wine with him, both of them from the same glass. She would play music, dance with him. She would kiss him, move her hands under his shirt, move her hips against his. Sit on his lap. Run her fingers through his hair.

All this she would do to make him forget, to make him love her even more than he did.

She looked at her face in the mirror. The sun had flushed her skin. Her eyes sparkled. She saw that she did not need much make-up. She applied an eyeliner and mascara and a neutral lip gloss. Her face looked fresh and naked, as though she had stepped out of a shower.

She chose to wear a white top with matching slacks. The outfit was loose and silky, suggesting her curves rather than clinging to her, just showing the lace bra beneath. There was a hint of innocence, a purity in the pearly silk. But her high-heeled silver sandals and the sway of her hips conflicted with this image, suggesting seduction, enhancing her sexuality.

She used her mother's perfume, a mature and heavy scent that she dabbed on her throat and wrists. She turned this way and that in front of her mirror and was satisfied.

Steve would like what he saw. Of that she was sure.

She then thought that perhaps, for fun, she would play the evening differently. Not fall all over him with kisses, but rather be somewhat cool. A little stand-offish. Make him do the chasing.

Yes. That's what she'd do. Sit opposite him. Smile and sip her wine and ask why he'd been so angry with her. Let him explain. Say that he didn't mean it. Keep him at arm's length. Perhaps even push him away a little… Then warm to him, slowly…slowly…so that he would be completely overcome with wanting her.

She opened the doors of the small informal lounge that faced the pool. The last rays of day filled the room with muted light. A pale oval moon hung low in the sky. There were the scents of honeysuckle and jasmine, the call of a bird, the shadows of moths in the terrace lights.

The house was quiet except for the padding of Chappie's paws. Carla was pleased to be on her own, pleased that she and Steve would be alone.

She prepared a plate of nuts and olives, and little round cheeses sealed in red and gold. She stood a bottle of good white wine next to two gleaming cut-glass goblets.

She chose to play Glenn Miller, turning the sound down so that it filtered as background music. She heard Chappie's bark, the thump of his tail on the floor.

Steve was at the front door.

It had been a difficult day for him. Distracted and ill at ease, he'd forced himself to focus on what he what he needed to say and how to say it.

Carla…

She'll be devastated. Heartbroken. Not only heartbroken. Humiliated and embarrassed to be ditched. Dumped by the man she passionately loved, by the man she'd said she would soon marry.

She'll be angry. Nasty. Vindictive.

Laura who, innocent though she was, might become the target of Carla's fury.

There was long-standing camaraderie between their families.

All their friends…

This was not going to be easy. Jeez…

He sighed, slipped his feet into old canvas shoes, ran his fingers through his hair, grabbed his car keys and drove to her house.

They faced each other in the fading light. She'd come to the door with her plan in place, to be cool and a little removed, but when she saw him she noticed immediately that something was wrong.

This was not the Steve she knew. She saw the bristles on his drawn face, his unsmiling eyes, a coffee stain on his sweater. He who was fastidious about his appearance, always immaculate and well groomed, was not the man who faced her.

'Steve,' she said softly and with concern, 'what is it? Are you not well?'

'Hi,' he answered. His voice sounded hoarse. 'I'm OK. But as I said, we need to talk…' He followed her down the passage without seeing her.

She turned to him. 'Would you like some wine? You can open the bottle…'

'No. I don't want wine.'

He stood apart from her with his back to the open door. She watched his face, trying to understand. Steve had never looked like this. He'd never behaved in this way. There's something really wrong, she thought. Something seriously wrong.

'Why don't you sit down?' She was alarmed. 'Tell me what's bothering you.'

'I don't want to sit…'

'Steve…' She moved towards him but his hands went up, keeping her away.

'Carla, I need to tell you something. I've given this a lot of thought. In fact, I haven't stopped thinking about it since last night. How to say this. How to tell you…

'Tell me what?' Her response was sharp. All her senses were alert. Her heart beat fast.

'I can't marry you. I know that's what you want. That you expect me to propose. But I can't do it.'

'How do you mean you can't marry me?'

'I just can't. I'm unsure of my feelings for you. I like you. I like you a lot. But I'm not in love with you…'

'You're not in love with me? Steve, we've been together for almost two years. We haven't dated anyone else in that time. You know how much I love you. You've never given me any reason to believe that you don't feel the same about me...'

'I know. Believe me, this isn't easy for me. It's probably the most difficult thing I've ever had to say. But I need to say it. I need to tell you that I'm not going ahead with this. Our relationship needs to end. We have to break it. To go our own ways.'

'Steve, I cannot believe what you're telling me!' Carla's voice was now raised. 'You come here and tell me, after nearly two years of being together, of being committed to each other, that we need to go our own ways. No! I won't accept this. You haven't thought this through. You're panicking because you think you have to propose to me now. You think you're not ready...'

'Carla, I hear everything you're saying. None of what you say applies. I don't want to proceed, because I'm not in love with you. The best thing is for us to break up, and to try and do it in a friendly and sensitive way...'

'What! Friendly? Sensitive? What are you saying? That you want to break up with me after all this time, and that you expect me to accept it in a friendly and sensitive way? That you're not in love with me? After being with me, only me, for two years?'

'I know this must be very hard for you, Carla. But I have to be honest. I have to tell you how I feel...'

'How you feel? What about the way I feel? Don't you know that you're the most important person in the whole world to me. That I cannot for one moment imagine my life without you?'

'I'm sorry, Carla. Really sorry. But there's really nothing more to be said. I won't be seeing you any more. I'm really sorry...'

Carla sank into the sofa, staring at him, her eyes bewildered. 'I can't believe what I'm hearing...that you're telling me this... After all this time... You can't mean it...'

He moved away from the terrace doors. 'I'm sorry. There's nothing more I can say. I have to go.'

'No, Steve.' She jumped up and clung to his arm. 'Please,' she begged. 'Please don't go.' Her face crumpled. Tears filled her eyes. 'Please don't leave me. Don't do this. I implore you. Don't leave me…'

He shook himself free of her grasp. 'I must go. I'm not coping too well myself. I need to leave. Now.' He walked swiftly down the passage.

'Steve,' she called after him. 'Steve. Please don't leave. Steve. Come back…'

She ran down the passage, out of the front door and down the steps. Tried to follow him, to catch up with him. But he was already far away from her.

She stood quite still, a ghostly figure in flowing white silk, alone in the empty driveway.

He drove through the streets, light to shadow, light to shadow. Numbly, he thought of how unsubstantial Carla had appeared to him at their meeting. A cardboard image of herself. How her words had floated. How her ravaged face had not registered with him. How her tears had no effect. How he'd been able to walk away from the two of them, from the two years that had passed.

He thought that he should have felt something. Remorse. Perhaps some regret. She was, after all, a lovely girl. Very much admired. Very much desired. He knew that she loved him. He was the one she wanted.

All this now seemed inconsequential. He'd walked away from her without a backward glance.

An image of Laura came to mind, vague and blurred. Perhaps she was simply a catalyst, someone who'd briefly come into his orbit to guide him out of an uncertain relationship.

These thoughts swirled through his mind on the short drive home, leaving him feeling light and strange, as though he, too, was made of cardboard.

Carla did not know how she managed to get back into the house. She stumbled down the passage, steadying herself against the wall. Stared unseeing into the darkness, at moving shadows.

Shocked. Unbelieving. Uncomprehending.

Steve doesn't want me. He doesn't want me, beating like a drum through her mind. Shivering uncontrollably, she fell into the couch.

Chappie watched her, his liquid eyes never leaving her face.

Two hours later, her parents found her curled into a foetal position, her hands held tightly between her knees, her face expressionless, her eyes blank.

She told them in gasping broken phrases in a high-pitched

hysterical voice, her face contorted, without lifting her head. Steve would not marry her. He thought it best they did not see each other.

They stood staring at her. Asking questions. Interrupting each other. Repeating the same questions. Over and over.

She screamed, 'Get away! Leave me alone!'

She twisted away from them, coiling into herself, the dog on the carpet beside her, his head on his paws, his eyes open. Every now and then, he would raise his head and look at her, hearing her sharp intake of breath, her disbelieving sobs.

Confused, agitated, not knowing what to do, they left her. Went to their bedroom.

They kept coming back, silently peering through the door. Throughout the night, they padded up and down the passage in bare feet.

Her mother, who was trying to give up, smoked one cigarette after another. 'How can he do this to her?' she kept asking, her eyes screwed up against the fumes. 'After all this time? Leading her on… Messing her around… For two years…'

He said, nervously pulling the sleeves of his pyjama top, 'I think he'll come back. Maybe he's not feeling well. He didn't look himself this afternoon. I think he'll think it through and realise what he's giving up. I mean, who wouldn't want Carla? She's so beautiful. A wonderful girl. I think he'll be back. But look what he's done. Look how upset she is. I mean, if this is what he's done now, maybe he's not right for her. Maybe even if he comes back, she shouldn't take him back… I mean, who does this? Who behaves like this? And his parents – our best friends for so many years. Since the kids were small. What will they say?'

'It's terrible. Absolutely terrible.' She lit one cigarette from the end of another.

'For God's sake! What are you doing? Look how you're smoking. The ashtray's full…'

'I don't care. I'm very upset.'

'So am I. But that doesn't mean you've got to smoke yourself to death.' His face crumpled.

He shook his head and went down the passage again. He saw that Carla had fallen into an uneasy sleep in the grey smudge of dawn. In her sleep, he heard her sob.

She phoned him the next day. His secretary said that he was in a meeting.

'It's urgent,' she said desperately. 'I have to speak to him!'

The woman asked her to hold the line, went away, returned and said that he was not available.

'How do you mean, not available? I have to speak to him!' she shouted into the receiver. She tried again. And again.

He did not take her call.

Barefoot, she paced through the house in trailing white silk, her eyes smudged with tears and mascara, her face contorted. Her mother followed, agitated and disturbed by her daughter's torment. She'd never seen Carla in such a state. Never seen her like this. Terrible. Absolutely terrible…

That night, Carla drove to his house.

His father came to the door. Saw her in bedraggled white silk, her white face ravaged. He tried to say, 'Sorry for the news.'

That did not sound right. Woodenly, he told her that Steve was not at home. He would tell him that she'd come. He saw the torture in her eyes, her downturned mouth, her agitated movements from one foot to the other.

Beside himself with concern for Carla, her father decided to take action. 'Leave this to me,' he told her mother, who was crying and shaking and wringing her hands.

He called Steve's father. Told him in a tense and tight voice that his daughter was devastated. Absolutely devastated. 'How could Steve do this to her?' he demanded. 'Speak to him,' he implored. 'He needs to make this right. He doesn't know what he's doing. She's madly in love with him. She never slept all night.' Neither had they. Nobody slept.

Steve's father said, without conviction, that he would try. For a while now, he'd suspected that, despite all their expectations, Steve would not go ahead with the engagement. He knew his son. He knew what he wanted. He did not vacillate. He would not proceed with something that he was not a hundred per cent sure of. Not their Steve.

But he said in a placating and conciliatory voice, 'I'll try. I'll see what I can do. I'll speak to him.'

Carla's heart was broken. She could not believe that Steve would not be her husband. Each day, she'd lived out her dream of being with him forever, of the house they would live in, of the children they would raise. These thoughts were deeply entrenched in her heart and in her mind.

She was sick with the realisation that none of this would happen.

She wandered hysterically round the house. Her heart cried out for Steve. She constantly called his name. In her bewildered state, she believed that he would come back to her. Every time the phone rang, she answered, thinking it was him. When the doorbell rang, she rushed barefoot to the door. She held his photograph. Would not let go of it.

Her mother never left the house. She remained a few steps away from her suffering child, who either screamed at her to go away or sobbed uncontrollably in her arms. Exhausted, the woman suffered through the torturous days, not knowing what to do or where to turn.

Her sister came. She adored Carla. She'd laughed at her caprices when they were children, and was intrigued with the cunning little wiles Carla had developed whilst growing up. She knew how much Carla loved Steve. How she'd schemed to ensnare him. How she'd worked at captivating him. The way she dressed, the expression in her eyes when she looked at him, the way she walked when he was watching her. She thought of how often Carla had told her, 'He's the only man for me. The only man in the whole world that I want.'

She also realised that it was not only losing Steve that was traumatising Carla. There were the friends. The so-called friends. Those girls who were jealous of her, who thought she showed off, who resented that she always seemed to get her own way. They were gossiping and sniggering, thinking and saying, 'Serves her right. She's such a spoilt brat!' behind her back.

Carla was well aware of their reactions, of their snide comments. She had often been nasty and malicious to others. For the first time in her life, she was on the receiving end – the object of their spiteful attention, their constant scrutiny. They were like cats licking cream.

She became pale. She lost weight. She lay on her bed with her face to the wall, or sat and stared listlessly at nothing.

Each day, her sister came.

Her mother hovered nervously.

Her aunts and uncles kept in constant touch. 'Don't worry…' they chorused.

'*Alles sal regkom*. Everything will come right,' from her uncle Sam, over and over.

'There are other fish in the sea,' said her uncle Mike.

'Bigger fish and better fish,' insisted Aunty Dora.

Aunty Bertha did what she did best, baked cakes. She told them that it was disgusting what Steve had done. Really disgusting. She'd never look at him again! If she saw him in the street, she'd walk right past him! Wouldn't so much as greet him. Honestly! He'd behaved disgracefully! And all that cheesecake he'd eaten. Never had any trouble eating her cheesecake when all the time he knew that he wasn't going to marry her niece.

They tried. They all tried, in a time of shock, of dreadful realisation, of intense loss.

A time that would not be hurried.

It was also a time of anger.

Furiously, Carla remembered Nigel's party. Laura. Did Steve phone her? Were they seeing each other?

She phoned Laura's house and demanded to speak to her. Was told that she was away. She wanted to know when Laura had left, when she was returning.

The man's voice became quiet. He wanted to know who was speaking.

'A friend,' she responded.

'Which friend?' he asked.

'It doesn't matter who I am,' she retorted.

'It certainly does,' he replied in the same quiet tone. 'I won't give you any information about my daughter until I know who you are.'

Carla replied, 'Oh, for God's sake! Forget it!' and banged down the receiver.

For Steve, the break-up was grim and challenging. He knew that there'd be extreme reactions.

The relationship between their families would be damaged. Their friends would be confused.

Carla had led everyone to believe that he would propose. They thought that he'd had made promises he'd broken.

'Not right what he's done,' they thought.

'Not the way to go.'

His parents continued to support him.

'It was not meant to be,' was his father's stock answer.

'Better the break-up now than later,' echoed his mother. 'You've got to be sure about marriage. It's got to be right. If it's not right, it can end up in divorce. No one would want that.'

She went on in this vein in her efforts to defend her son, but she was not convinced. She'd thought that Steve and Carla were beautiful together. A lovely couple. Perfectly suited. She tried to talk to Steve, tell him that maybe he was making a mistake.

Her husband told her to leave him alone. 'He knows what he's doing. He's old enough to make up his own mind. Stop nagging him,' he told her.

Steve knew that Carla was suffering.

He asked himself how he had remained involved with her for so long. What it was that had intrigued him? He recalled her eyes, her smile, the fullness and slenderness of her. The love that radiated from her for him.

But that brief encounter with Laura had shaken him out of his reverie. He was not in love with Carla. That was the truth of the matter.

He faced the accusations levelled at him, the judgements, the condemnation. 'Well, that's how it is,' he'd reply with a grave expression in his eyes.

To escape their censure and to block his own unease, he threw himself into his work, was at the office before he needed to be, remained long after his work was done. He tried to burn his discomfort by running around the sports field, by swimming laps in the pool.

He spent his evenings and weekends at home, reading but not absorbing the words on the page, listening to music without hearing the notes.

He deeply regretted the upset and pain he'd caused Carla. He regretted the damage done to the long-standing friendship between their families. He was sorry that it hadn't worked.

But he knew that he'd done the right thing. The only thing he could have done.

The only person who understood and accepted his decision without question was his brother Nigel.

Laura faced the sea. She closed her eyes to the breeze, felt it caress her face, lift her hair. It was a breeze from the ocean's far horizons, warmed by the sun, flirting with the waves, making them sparkle, making them dance.

She went down the long line of hewn steps to the beach, dropped her bag and towel on the hot sand and walked into the shallow lapping water. Here the sand was smooth and silky. It separated and closed over her feet. Slowly she went forward, catching her breath in the cold Atlantic sea.

She'd wanted the morning to herself. She needed time to think. Away from the crowd.

The sun warmed her tanned body and tinged her face. She closed her eyes against the white glare of the sea and sand.

Immediately, Steve came into her thoughts. His eyes sparkled. His smile gleamed. He was never far from her. His image came to her during the day and in her dreams.

She told herself that she shouldn't be thinking of him. He belonged to someone else. He was about to get engaged. They might have made the announcement already.

She remembered his broad shoulders, the French knot in his tie.

She wondered what on earth had happened that evening that had such an effect on her. After all, it was only a few fleeting moments. An exchange of glances, smiles, some words. That was all.

What took place between them in that brief encounter that had flickered and now flamed inside her? What was this feeling that kept coming to her? This warm wanting of someone she did not know.

Laura was hot and uncomfortable. She sat up and lifted her hair from the back of her neck. Again she'd allowed herself to indulge in images of Steve. She was being ridiculous. This had to stop.

The long curve of white beach seemed barren and lonely. The sea stretched monotonously. The sky was flat and lifeless.

She no longer wanted to be alone. Impatiently, she threw her towel over her shoulder, climbed the long flight of steps and quickly walked back along the promenade.

She needed a cappuccino. She needed to be with her friends.

In the weeks that followed the break-up, Steve maintained a low profile. This was not deliberate. It was out of need. He'd taken a serious decision and had acted upon it. In the process, he'd hurt and upset many people. He'd damaged relationships. He'd broken Carla's heart. He felt depleted.

On impulse, he booked a flight to London.

'Freezing at this time of the year,' remarked his dad, looking at him quizzically.

'Slushy,' said his mother.

'Mushy,' from his brother.

But he went anyway. He needed to be away from the summer heat, the people, the pools and the parties.

He walked the streets of London in a heavy overcoat and a thick scarf, his breath steaming, his hands deep in his pockets. Preferring to be alone, he sipped tea, staring out of streaked windows at the streets of black umbrellas. It was endlessly grey, dismal and cold, but Steve became peaceful in the anonymity and aloneness in which he was immersed.

He went to museums and art galleries. He sat in matinee shows, came out to the murky dusk, walked through the penetrating fog to his hotel.

He watched the television. Read the newspapers. Ate dinner in his room. Went to bed early and slept long and well.

He did not think of Carla.

He would not allow himself to think of Laura.

He waited. Let the days pass, one into the next, without taking note, until one morning he woke, looked out of the window at the shifting river below, and knew that it was time to go home.

It was her sister who suggested that Carla contact her previous boyfriend, Ian. 'Give him a ring. It's ages since you've seen him.'

Ian had been in love with Carla since she was twelve years old. His mother used to laugh and tell her friends, 'That girl is my future daughter-in-law.' As soon as they were old enough, they became boyfriend and girlfriend. Went everywhere hand in hand. Then Carla decided that they should not go steady. They should still see each other but also go out with others. It was not what Ian wanted but he had no choice. He agreed 'to cool it for a while'.

The relationship waxed and waned. Ian's mother stopped referring to Carla as her future daughter-in-law. She began to dislike the spoilt capricious girl. She hoped that her son would find someone more worthy of him.

But he did take to Carla to his graduation party and the love he had for her shone from his eyes. The next day he sent her a bouquet of roses with a note that said, 'I hope to send you roses forever.'

It was not long after this that Carla began to date Steve.

He was terse when he heard her voice. He'd heard that she was going to marry Steve. That had been very difficult for him to process. Carla was entrenched in his heart. But his work kept him busy, and a colleague, a girl who had gone through medical school with him, had been a constant and warm friend for whom he had great affection.

He knew he needed to move on. He thought that this was happening, that he was getting over her. Until he heard her voice again.

The girl who came into his dreams…

'Carla.'

'Ian…'

Silence. Then, 'How are you?'

'I'm OK.'

'You sound surprised.'

'I am surprised.'

'I know. We haven't spoken for a while...'

Ian ran his fingers through his dark hair. 'Carla, why are you phoning me? I heard you were practically engaged... To Steve.'

'Engaged?' There was a break in her voice. 'No. I'm not engaged. We've broken up. I thought you might have heard.'

Again there was a pause.

'So.' Ian was apprehensive. 'You've broken up.'

'Yes. It's over. And you? Are you involved with anyone?'

'I have been seeing someone.'

'Are you getting engaged?'

Carla. Her dark eyes. Her smile. She came back to him in an overwhelming surge of emotions. All of her. She enveloped him. As always, she swamped his being with her image, the sound of her voice.

'No. I'm not getting engaged.' His reply was cautious.

'Perhaps we could see each other again. Have a coffee together.' She seemed warm and encouraging.

He thrilled to the sound of her. 'I don't know... I don't know what to say...'

'Don't say anything,' Carla answered gently. 'Think about it. Give me a ring if you want to see me...if you want to catch up... Give me a ring some time...'

The wedding surpassed everyone's expectations.

Carla's parents were determined show to their guests how absolutely delighted they were with their new son-in-law, how nothing was too grand for their beautiful daughter. How, actually, in the end, everything had turned out for the best.

The licking of wounds, the embarrassment, the recriminations, were now a thing of the past. Who remembered Steve? Who missed him?

There were those who remembered. The whispered comments.

Those who said Ian had caught Carla on the rebound, those who thought she'd gone back to him, not because she really loved him, but to move on with her life and put her heartache behind her.

'For Carla, this is a marriage of convenience,' was a statement made by one of her closest friends.

But as the young couple took to the floor for their first dance, the bride exquisite in capure lace, her husband handsome and elegant in his evening suit, none could deny that they made the perfect couple.

None, that is, except for the groom's mother. Her dislike of Carla could not be disguised. She was bitterly disappointed that her son had gone back to 'that little so 'n' so'. She'd loved the young doctor with whom he was previously linked. 'A wonderful girl. Lovely. From such a lovely family.' How he chose Carla over her she could not fathom.

She was also afraid for her son, afraid that he was throwing his life away on this awful girl who had messed him around for years. Terrified that he would again be hurt. Her wonderful son. Her beautiful boy.

In the months that followed, Carla and Ian moved to London. He was going to specialise in neurology. She was going to have her first baby.

On a cold winter's night with leaves brushing against the window panes, Steve phoned.

They had dinner together. They looked deeply into each other's eyes. They smiled. They held hands. They awoke to the feelings they'd felt for each other the night they met. It was love. Love before they knew each other. Love that grew and deepened with the time that they shared.

'I'm so much in love with you,' he told her. 'I love everything about you. I envy the years I didn't know you…'

They met her family.

'Ordinary people,' is how his mother described them.

'Nice people,' said her dad. 'Good people.'

'No money,' her mother told her friends. 'But,' in a rush, and as an afterthought, 'she's a lovely girl. Clever. Well educated.'

To herself, she thought, not sure what he sees in her. Carla would have been a better choice.

To her sister she said, 'You can't choose for them. Not who I thought he'd end up with. But it's his decision. His life.'

The wedding was a modest affair on a Sunday afternoon. Laura looked ethereal in white silk with flowers in her hair. She'd chosen the same waltz that her parents had had all those years before.

> I'll be loving you always
> With a love that's true always
> When the things you've planned
> Need a helping hand
> I will understand always always
> Things may not be fair always
> That's when I'll be there always
> Not for just an hour

Not for just a day
Not for just a year
But always…

Laura came out of the bathroom wrapped in two towels, one around her body, the other twisted into a turban around her wet hair.

The girls had left for school, Steve for his office.

The house quietly settled. The clouds had disappeared. Through the windows, pale slabs of light entered the rooms. On the patio, clusters of mauve wisteria glowed like amethysts.

A squirrel ran across the lawn. It was quite tame, sitting up as if to greet her, but it came because of the almond tree.

She undid the turban, rubbed the drops from her hair, shook it into a mass of auburn waves, felt the warmth of the sun on her face, saw the bright tumble of the garden facing her.

Breathing in the mixed scents of flowers and herbs, she was filled with pleasure, with joy, and with an excited sense of creativity.

Slipping into comfortable slacks and a loose sweater, she tied her damp hair back and sat at her desk. She was hopeful that something would happen today. That there would be words she would want to keep.

Steve never thought about his love for Laura. If asked how married life was treating him, he would reply, 'Beautiful. Laura, she's beautiful. In every way. It's beautiful to come home to her.'

If he'd given it thought, he'd have realised that with Laura peace had entered his life. Her beauty was steeped in gentility and quietude. She spoke in mellow tones, moved with grace, radiated serenity. These qualities permeated their home and their lives. After the stress of a business day and the frustrations that often frazzled his nerves, he drove home along tree-lined streets, remembered his wife and became calm.

Holding her gave him comfort. She was slight in his arms. Delicate. Her hands were gentle, her kiss tender. The perfume that she used was light and subtle, seeming to come from the very essence of her. She'd hold his face in her hands, look deeply into his eyes searching for how his day had gone, whether it had been difficult or confronting, and with her eyes willed love and comfort to him.

She would tell him of her day, of what the girls had been up to, of something funny that had happened. Sitting opposite him on the sofa with legs folded, she smiled and waited. Always waited to accommodate his needs, offering words of advice if he asked, remaining silent if he did not. She did not intrude, but was there, a passive and serene presence.

Steve was not conscious of this. He only knew that he was happy to come home, looked forward to being with Laura and delighting in the company of his two daughters.

The house reflected Laura. Situated in a quiet cul-de-sac in a good area, it was an attractive but unassuming single storey with white walls and a black slate roof in a green garden filled with a profusion of sweet smelling shrubs and flowers, fruit trees, pungent herbs and fecund vegetable patches.

In the bright and flowing rooms, they could easily find each other.

But it was the kitchen, a living breathing space, that belonged to all of them. A place with a big wooden table where homework was done, pictures were drawn and stories were written. A place that was filled with the smell of a rich roast, and the sounds of soup bubbling. Where they ate in the bright warm light of day and the white light of moon and stars. A place that happily accommodated their dog, a stray kitten, a bird with a torn wing.

There was also the music. It filtered through the house softly, harmoniously, without intruding. Outside were the birds, the chirping of crickets, the buzzing of bees, the shushing of the leaves. Peace and warmth and light.

A reflection of the essence of Laura.

She sat at the kitchen table and wrote.

She read the words.

She scratched out words. She deleted sentences.

She put a pencil through paragraphs.

She crunched paper into balls.

She started again.

And again.

Each day, she devoted time trying to write. Each day, she formed ideas, made notes, created scenarios.

She knew what she wanted to say. How she wanted to say the words. But there was something fundamental missing.

The children's stories were doing well. The tales she'd made up and told the girls each evening as they snuggled into bed had been transformed into a successful series of books that was selling well. But their daughters were older now. They were reading books. The time of making up and telling stories for them was past.

That time had also passed for Laura. She was trying to write a novel. She had the characters, she'd formed a plot in her mind, she knew how it should look, how it should sound. But the substance remained elusive.

She remembered the words of her lecturer. He'd told them to keep notes. To observe. To absorb. To use all their senses, and also their instincts.

'This will give you what you're looking for – more meaning, more depth…'

She had always observed. Even as a child, she preferred to watch and listen. Her mother had kept her nursery school reports that reported, 'An observer rather than a participant' when it came to activities.

She had images in her mind. She had to find a way to convert them to words on the page. In the meantime, there were the short stories. There was also a small collection of published poems.

She phoned her professor, her mentor, who believed she showed promise. Who told her that she would succeed.

'It's hopeless,' she complained. 'It's not coming together. I know what I want to say. I know my characters. But they aren't coming through as genuine. They sound so contrived.'

He listened to how the plot had no sense of climax, how it read as laboured and boring. How the story had no depth of feeling. How she was losing heart. Was wondering whether she should continue. Whether writing was really her vocation. He heard her say that she loved writing, but, honestly, it was such hard work!

'Laura,' he counselled, 'What do you expect? You're young. How can you hope to have depth of feeling when you haven't experienced life? Writers need to feel things deeply. That comes with maturity. It comes from going through trials and tribulations that the writer internalises, and is then able to be expressed through the different characters.

'If you're a serious writer, not a writer of light romance, you'll have to be patient. Read. Read the Nobel prize winners, the French writers, the Russians. You'll get a feel for the depths of feelings they express through their characters.

'If you're serious about becoming a novelist, you have to have patience. It's a craft practised over many years, combined with accumulated obser-vations, sensitivities and feelings, all of which are implicit in the writer.

'Don't give up, my dear. I believe you have ability. Give it time. Years, if necessary. Life will teach you. The years will give you the tools to reach the goals you want. I feel sure that ultimately you will create something that you will be proud of. Don't give up, my dear Laura. Don't give up.'

The first photographs of the girls were as small as they were, in black and white. Babies in prams wearing pretty crocheted jackets made by Laura's mother, staring at the lens uncomprehendingly. Sometimes they'd been able to catch a smile. There's one of Arielle holding a rattle, another of Carolyn drinking from her bottle. Their first steps. Their toes dipping in the swimming pool. Eating ice cream, smudges on their cheeks and chins and fingers. Images of the girls in the speech eisteddfods, the ballet concerts… And, of course, the handkerchief dance.

Laura remembered how she used to take them to her parents' home. How she herself needed to go back there. She recalled the plain square house, the stiff little path leading up red cement steps to the front door with a knocker in the shape of a dog's head, the covered *stoep*, the kitchen. The smell of cooking that came to greet them, the sound of chatter, her mother's laugh. The radio. Always the radio. The news. Her mother's serials. A Frank Sinatra song…

Her dad in his shirt sleeves at the kitchen table, reading the newspaper. Her mother at the stove making soup, or a stew. Perhaps a chicken in the oven. On the table a steaming teapot in a blue crocheted cover, the aroma of tea wafting. The square cake tin with the imprint of a cottage surrounded by hollyhocks in which was a fruitcake rich with currents and cherries. Their hugs, their smiles, the bits of news her father shared with them, her mother's laugh.

The girls were little enough to play in the garden, picking flowers and climbing the ancient fig tree.

'Why does Grandpa paint the trunk?' asked Carolyn.

'To keep the ants away,' said Granny.

In the cold weather, they would unpack the handkerchief drawer, be quiet for ages, then come into the kitchen dressed in handkerchiefs that they had knotted together to make skirts and bandanas. Kerchiefs were tied around their necks. They made bracelets of the lace-trimmed ones, and sometimes tied long tails of knotted hankies behind them.

Giggling, they would announce, 'We're going to sing and dance for you!' and cavort around the kitchen singing ditties they'd made up.

Around they would go until Laura, laughing, said, 'That's enough, girls,' and, giggling, they would bow to resounding applause.

Once, they included the cat, tying a hanky around his neck, but when they tried to tie one around his tail, he'd yowled and stalked off indignantly.

'Hold still,' Laura had laughed. 'Ready? Cheese…' and took the photograph.

On wet days, they'd curl up on Laura's bed and read Grimm's *Fairy Tales* and Hans Christian Andersen, or lie on the carpet piecing a puzzle together.

They visited every Saturday afternoon while Steve slept.

One day, Carolyn announced that she did not want to go. 'There's nothing to do there,' she stated. 'It's boring.'

At the back of the album, as in all the albums, was the exercise book containing her notes, her observations and her descriptions – the colours, the tastes, the smells… What she'd seen and what she'd heard. How she'd felt.

The first note in the book at the back of one of the albums reads, 'I really don't want to go. I don't want to leave the children. Arielle is only eight. I know they'll be OK but she's very young to be without me for six whole weeks. Six weeks! Such a long time! I really wish we didn't have to go…'

They drove the children, together with their trusted maid Rosie and their suitcases, to Steve's parents. Arielle clung to Laura all the way. She was sobbing, begging her mother not to go. Promises of presents and regular phone calls did nothing to comfort her.

But a firm 'Arielle, it's enough now. Stop snivelling' from Steve caused her to stop, to pull away from Laura and stare straight ahead, her arms tightly folded.

Steve's parents were there to greet them. They stood on the steps in the driveway and waved the car away, except for Arielle, who clutched Rosie's hand. Her small face was twisted in anguish.

Distressed, Laura turned to catch a last glimpse of her. I know how you feel, darling, she said silently. I don't want to go either. I don't want to leave you… But Dad wants this trip and I have to go with him. I hope when you're older you'll understand.

Her notes said that by the time they reached the airport, she was excited. The children would be fine. They were well looked after. And her mother would be in touch. She knew that.

Steve was right. They needed to get away, spend time together, just the two of them.

They walked through duty-free hand in hand. He bought her perfume. Now he was looking at the jewellery, at the black pearls.

The flight took her away, enchanting her, with its way of turning day into night, then sunrise blazing over mountains, then impenetrable cloud (how could the pilot see where to go?), then washed blue skies and Tel Aviv airport. There was the playing of the national anthem as the El Al plane landed in Israel, the Holy Land. Laura felt her throat swelling. Her eyes filled with tears. A man walking ahead of them knelt down and kissed the ground.

Steve's relatives made their assessments. Thought she was pretty and sweet, but young. Much younger than him. A bit innocent, they thought – how they say? Naive? And him so sophisticated. The women, confident and assertive, were charmed by Steve, smiled at him, watched him with suggestive eyes and engaging smiles.

Laura noticed. She also saw how easily Steve fitted into this urbane crowd who spent time in Rome and Paris, who were conversant with opera and classical music, with theatre and musicals. Who read voraciously. More importantly, who understood their own culture, their country, their country's needs, their country's politics. Whose children went into the army, fought wars, defended their borders. They all knew someone whose son who had been killed. Someone who was forever maimed. Beneath the charm and *savoir faire* they had suffered. But they were tough. *Sabras*, born into wars, striving, surviving and overcoming. Successful hard-boiled people made up of many parts.

They seemed to understand Steve. He related to them. Laura was out of their realm.

'What are you scribbling?' Steve asked when they came back to their hotel.

'Nothing,' she replied. 'Nothing important,' covering her observations.

He wouldn't understand, she thought. For the first time since they married, she felt their differences. Felt that she was removed from him.

For Steve, it was good to be in Israel again. He loved the country. He was fond of his relatives. They were clever, stimulating and exciting people. He was intrigued with their wives, fascinating flirtatious women who held his arm or placed an intimate hand on his shoulder. They showed their admiration for him and he was flattered by their warm smiles and laughing eyes.

He wished that Laura was more forthcoming in their company. She faded into the background, seemed lost and bewildered among these women in their exotic clothes and flamboyant jewellery.

'You have to admire them.' He spoke with enthusiasm, with admiration. 'Nothing gets them down. All the wars. The sacrifices they have to make. They deal with everything in such an amazing way. Live for the day. Live for the moment. Amazing people, these Israelis…' He paused.

'Did you enjoy yourself?' he asked cautiously.

'Yes.' She hesitated. 'It was very nice. I got a bit lost when they spoke Hebrew. I mean, you're OK because you understand it, can speak it, but I don't.'

'They didn't speak Hebrew all the time. They tried to accommodate you.'

'I know. They did try. They are nice.'

'Well, I had a great time.' He yawned and turned on his side. 'Sleep well,' he said automatically and was instantly asleep.

He saw the dress in the window. It was in shades of pinks and fuchsia. 'Come,' he said, excited. 'I like that dress. I want you to try it on.'

'Steve, it's not really my colour.'

'How do you mean, not your colour? How do you know until you've tried it on?'

She came out of the change room in the slim-fitting dress. It had a low neckline and a slit up the back of the skirt. It clung to her body, revealing the shape of her bust, the curve of her behind. It was not the sort of dress that Laura would have bought herself. She was self-conscious.

She watched Steve's face.

His eyes shone. 'Wow!' he exclaimed softly. 'You look amazing, darl! You look absolutely amazing!'

'I don't know, Steve. It's not really my taste.'

'Then change your taste. Go with the times. This is the sort of dress women are wearing. It looks great on you.'

'Do you really think so? I don't know…'

'Come on, Laura. Lighten up. Get with it.' He turned to the shop attendant. 'We'll take it,' he said. 'Looks great. Amazing. Really suits you. We'll take it.'

I've seen a side to Steve that I never knew, she'd written. I notice that he's really excited by certain types of women, overt women with suggestive eyes. Women who are not shy to show him that they're attracted to him. Who encourage him to flirt with them.

I notice, her notes said sadly, that he responds to that type of attention without reserve, without remembering me. Without recalling that he's married, that they are married.

When he's in that environment, I don't exist for him.

He was more himself in Italy.

Entranced, they walked through the ancient city, the Colosseum, the Roman Forum, the Pantheon, the Piazza Navona, Galleria Borghese. They threw coins into the Trevi Fountain, held hands and declared their love for each other, promised that their love was forever, that their souls were bound together, that, hand in hand, they would walk into eternity. Looking deeply into each other's eyes, they made these vows to each other, and were overwhelmed by their love in this immensely beautiful and timeless place.

They saw the pope on his balcony in the Vatican City and felt the adoration of the crowd for someone who represented a religion different from their own. They'd just left the tiny country of Israel with its fervour for Jehovah. Here was fervour for Jesus Christ through the Roman Catholic Church.

I've witnessed the power of religion, Laura wrote. The power of belief in a higher being. The radiance it brings. It doesn't matter, she philosophised in her notes, what your religion. What matters is faith. To believe…

They travelled on a bus to Sorrento, in a bus that negotiated the twists and turns of the road at terrifying speed, roads so narrow they could have touched the passing houses. In a boat that rode the waves into the Blue Grotto with a boatman who sang love songs, his rich voice swelling in that eerie light.

Then Capri, and Anacapri past Gracie Fields' house. Steve sang, his beautiful voice filling the bus space with words from a song she used to sing,

> When I grow too old to dream
> I'll have you to remember
> When I grow too old to dream
> Your love will live in my heart

Laura was overcome with sadness. She did not know why.

They came to the Villa San Michele, the home of Axel Munthe, Swedish physician and author. They walked through the pergola with its ancient statue, the loggia, the chapel. Enthralled, she thought of his book *The Story of San Michele.*

One day, I will write a book, she promised herself. I will try and write so that people remember me as I remember Axel Munthe.

In Paris, Steve's mood changed again.

They were on an organised tour, locked in with a crowd of tourists from different countries.

There was a young couple from Ireland who, it soon became abundantly clear, were disenchanted with each other. The husband was brooding and moody. His wife was overtly happy, as though to compensate for his unfriendliness. She was a pretty girl with eyes like emeralds and a mass of uncontrollable dark curls. Her mouth was red and moist and her teeth white and wet. She liked to lick her lips and touch a dimple in her cheek as though to draw attention to it. She seemed to be always moving, twisting her body, rocking her crossed leg. She talked and laughed and leaned between Steve and Laura from her seat behind them on the bus, her arm touching the back of Steve's neck. There was her perfume, her shifting breasts under her silk shirt, her voice that was musical, but sometimes breathy.

There was her interest in Steve. There was his ready response.

All he had to do was ignore her, Laura wrote in a locked bathroom at the hotel. If he took no notice of her, she would have turned her attentions elsewhere. But all the time he watched her. It was obvious that he liked what he saw.

Should I say something? she queried in her notebook.

'How old are you?' she asked.

The girl simpered.

Laura turned to Steve. 'Twenty-three,' she repeated. 'You're old enough to be her father,' she smiled sweetly.

Again she was unhappy. Ill at ease. Did not know how to cope with her dilemma.

If she challenged him, he could become angry. Turn on her. She would not be able to handle that. I wish it was over. That we were back home again. The sooner this trip comes to an end, she'd written, the better.

Dusk entered the study. The trees became shadows. A frog croaked. Steve said it wasn't a frog. How could a frog live without water? But there was one who must have lived in a drain and perhaps swam in the gutters after the rain.

In the dim light, Laura remembered. She turned on a lamp and read her notes about the Israeli women, flamboyant and exuberant. How intrigued they'd been with Steve. How he'd responded to their attentions. She now wondered whether he'd been flattered by them or whether he had given the signals.

She wondered why it was that there were a few men in that

company who had not been drawn into flirtations, who maintained their status as respectable married men. Why there were others who played the games, who imagined that they were young unencumbered boys again.

She'd heard about couples throwing their front door keys into a hat, of men drawing out a key and going home with the wife of the man whose key it belonged to. She would not have been surprised if some in that crowd of accomplished successful people had reached a level of boredom that compelled them to look for other diversions.

What had hurt her was how readily Steve seemed to fit in with the latter group, the men-boys… She knew that these games was not for her. There had been men who found her attractive, who smiled at her and looked at her from across a room, but she never responded.

She never would. She was only interested in one man. Steve.

She wrote about the Irish girl with green eyes like agate and dark bouncing curls. Why had she made a play for Steve? Why did he take note of her?

What happened between men and women that was said without words? What occurred that aroused the senses and became irresistible, irrespective of the status of these men and women? What made them cross boundaries when they were married? When their spouses would be hurt in the process?

She wrote that it seems that while it lasts this process is very powerful. It is persistent and focused, steamrolling over all in its path. It surges uncontrollably. It takes over men and women, irrespective of their partners at their sides.

She had sensed this in Steve and the Irish girl. It lasted throughout the two-day bus tour in Paris. These two strangers, years apart and with little in common, had recognised, if only in their minds, an irresistible attraction between them, and had allowed themselves to indulge in the thrill of their flirtation.

She wondered about Steve. Where did this come from? Was it hereditary?

His father was what her mother called 'a charmer'. Always dapper in his three-piece suits with a folded white hanky in the breast pocket, kissing the cheeks of women, holding their arms as he escorted them into or out of their house. Was his dad like that?

Perhaps, she wrote, it was a need for attention.

Were her attentions not enough for him? He knew that she loved him, that she was devoted to him and their girls, that they were her first priority. She knew that he loved her, that he found her beautiful. He said that he loved her. He often made love to her.

He spoilt and indulged her far more than she ever wanted or desired. Perhaps, her notes summarised, that is how some men are? Perhaps some men need constant endorsement of their prowess.

Perhaps they constantly need to prove to themselves that they are still attractive to other women. That's how Steve seemed to be.

It worried her. Perhaps she wasn't that attractive to him after all?

She paged through the albums. She wanted to remember. To record.

She wrote of ballet shoes.

Castanets.

Cast on arm (with loving messages).

The egg race.

Ice creams on the beach.

Trixie arrives.

The school dance.

First prize.

Again first prize.

Of Carolyn and Arielle, she wrote

Tightly curled buds

Unfurl

Blush

Full-blown flowers

Bloom

Flush

Of Steve

How far we are from where we were

How wide the ways between us

You fall asleep, your back to me

You fall asleep before me

Of herself

Those flimsy seasons

How brief how fleeting

An image a dream
A moment speeding

She wondered
    Will we always love as we have loved
    Will we always be loved as we've been loved
    Will we be strong if on our own
    Will we be strong if all alone

The study was bathed in late summer sun. On the terrace, fallen leaves rustled. Laura was folded into the couch, again looking at the wedding photos.

How beautiful Carolyn was. Laura could not help but be in awe of their elder daughter. The image faced her – slender, elegant, her blonde hair swept up, the finely chiselled bones of her face, her lovely smile. She was like Steve, not only in her look, but in her manner. She had his confidence and his relaxed approach that belied his focus and determination to succeed.

And succeed he did, becoming a leading property developer and, in the process, a wealthy man.

He'd insisted that they move out of their first house, the house that Laura loved, and into a mansion that he'd designed and built.

He made sure that they had the right friends, wealthy successful people who travelled extensively. Two of them owned ocean-going yachts that cruised the Mediterranean. Although Laura was not interested, he thought that he, too, might buy a yacht.

Carolyn, recently qualified as a doctor, married a young cardiologist. In her meticulous way, she'd seen to all the wedding details – the invitations, the lists of guests, the ceremony, the venue, the choice of band, the flowers. She designed her dress and chose her retinue. Of course, in Carolyn's hands, it had been perfect and breathtakingly beautiful.

Now the young couple were gone to a new life in another country. As they left, Carolyn's departing words were, 'Remember, Ma. The photo albums are mine…'

The late afternoons were tedious.

Steve came home late.

Arielle was studying in her room.

The cook was preparing dinner.
The housemaid was folding the washing.
The gardener was watering the plants.
She yawned and stretched.
She looked at her watch.
It was only five o'clock.
She sighed.
There was nothing for her to do.

Laura was up with the glorious summer dawn. Blooms opened their faces to the sun that was a brilliant yellow disc in an immaculate sky. Perfumes hung in the air. Dew sparkled.

All was perfect. A perfect day.

She stood barefoot on the terrace, in awe of the crisp morning. There was a feeling of anticipation, of unbridled joy that came from within her and seemed to surround her.

Arielle was getting married today. Her younger daughter. Her baby. Arielle. Shy. Retiring. Clever but modest. Sweet and good. Humble. Always in the background.

A lot like her mom, people said. Carolyn's like Steve. Arielle's exactly like her mom.

Laura wasn't sure that this was a compliment.

But her sensitive daughter was fulfilled, quietly happy and content. She'd completed an arts degree, had majored in English, was a creative writer and a talented artist.

The man she was marrying was her exact opposite. Exuberant, commanding, ambitious, he was a young barrister who was gaining a formidable reputation. Although he'd only known Arielle for a few months when he proposed, he'd fallen in love with her immediately. Her quiet beauty, sweet nature and gentle manner had captivated him. He was entranced with the pale creaminess of her skin, her green eyes, her mass of auburn hair, her soft full mouth, her lovely smile.

Her slimness and her daintiness. Her unobtrusive way of entering a room, of sitting upright in a chair. The turn of her head, the folding her pretty hands. Her soft musical voice. The way she listened rather than talked. The way she listened with her eyes. The way she understood. The way she loved. Her warmth. Her soft and affectionate touch.

They bloomed and blossomed together.

It was in the White Garden that the photographs of the bride and her retinue were taken, a place that Laura had made her own, where she'd planted white blooms and flowering shrubs. An ornamental bench and wrought-iron table holding a pot of miniature white roses stood in green shade, under trees that screened this secret corner of the garden that was concealed behind the summer house.

Laura, in rose chiffon, quietly watched Arielle pose for the various shots. She thought that her daughter looked breathtakingly pure. Exquisite.

She did not want to. She dared not. Her mascara…

But she did. She could not help herself.

She began to cry.

The house felt empty. Arielle and her husband had also emigrated after their wedding. For a few days following their departure, there were echoes of the *simcha*, the celebration.

Wedding cake. Flowers from the reception. Arielle's dress and veil. Her bouquet drying on her dressing table.

There were gifts that needed to packed and sent across the seas. There were things to be done.

Laura would see to them.

As the days passed, the presence of Arielle, her voice and her laugh and her light footsteps faded.

Steve went to work.

The maids talked in the kitchen.

The dog barked.

The lawnmower chugged.

But for Laura the house was silent.

What was encouraging was her writing. It was beginning to flow. She had a storyline. She was developing the characters.

She created a firm routine, sitting each morning in the small lounge, a space that she'd made her own. French doors to the terrace opened to sun and air, to the sounds and scents of the garden, enabling her to shut herself away from the house that held no interest for her, that she disliked.

Perhaps now that the girls were gone, Steve would consider selling and moving into something more suitable for the two of them.

Her hairdresser told her that Carla and Ian had returned some months before. They'd bought a house two suburbs away. People were bumping into them everywhere. At the supermarket. In a restaurant. Outside the pharmacy.

They came across each other in the shopping centre.

Carla said, 'Hi, Laura. It's been a long time. You're looking well.'

'Thanks.' Laura was reserved. 'I heard you were back.'

They watched each other.

'How've you settled?'

'It's taken a while but we're pleased to be back. Our main concern was the children. But they've taken to everything like ducks to water.' She smiled warmly. 'How many do you have?'

'Two. Two girls.'

'Two girls? Any weddings?'

'Yes. They're both married. And you? Do you have married children?'

'Our daughter. She got married a year ago. They're in London.'

'You must miss her.'

'Terribly. We speak every day.'

Laura found herself responding spontaneously. Thoughts of her daughters disarmed her. 'I know how you feel. Both our girls emigrated after their weddings.'

'Both? That must be hard for you.'

'It is. The house is empty. We both feel it. Such a strange empty feeling,' Laura confided.

Carla reached out to touch her hand. 'I'm so pleased to see you again.' She sounded sincere.

'I bumped into Carla today,' she told Steve.

'How was it?' He glanced up from reading the newspaper.

'Fine. She was quite friendly.'

'Well, it's been a long time. We've all moved on.'

They met again across a dinner table.

She saw that his hair was tinged with grey but that his eyes were the same shade of blue, his smile the same as that smile that had captivated her when they were young.

He thought, she looks great.

Carla's short dark curls. Her shimmering eyes. Her glittering smile. The soft fullness of her neck and arms, her smooth shoulders and her fuller breasts. Her small restless hands, her crimson-tipped nails. The sparkle of diamonds.

In her animated way, she spoke of London. Loved the theatre. Hated the weather. Regular escapes to Spain and the South of France. The Riviera. Loved the Riviera. Ian paid attention, his dark eyes focused on Steve. Steve listened and nodded. His eyes moved over her, meeting her flirting eyes over the rim of her glass.

They smiled for each other.

Ian leaned forward, his face stern, his arm possessively around Carla, fingering her arm, and asked in deliberate tones. 'And how are things with you, Steve? Hear the business is doing well.'

Tearing his eyes from her, Steve turned to Laura. He heard her voice but not what she was saying. He poured another glass of wine, talked too much and laughed too loudly.

'She looks lovely,' was Laura's comment.

'She looks OK,' was his. 'Put on a bit of weight.' He was aware of the stirrings within him.

'You seemed quite taken up with her.' Laura's voice was timid.

'Don't overblow it.' His response was brusque. 'I was just being friendly.'

A friend mentioned that Carla and Ian were doing alterations to their house, something about adding on a conservatory, 'For her orchids. She grows orchids. I heard that Steve's company was doing the job.'

'Are you?'

'What?'

'Doing their job?'

'Their job?'

'Yes. Their job.'

'Yes,' he said. They'd contacted him a couple of months ago. In fact, the work was almost complete.

Laura wondered. Such a small job, she thought. Why would his company be doing it? A hothouse. Why's he building them a hothouse? She was uneasy. She'd seen how they looked at each other at the dinner party.

She wanted to ask more questions but his face was closed. Leave it alone, she told herself. She forced herself to return to her manuscript, trying to focus on to the words.

Steve had decided not to send the foreman. He would go. He was curious. He wanted to talk to her, to find out about her life.

She was surprised to see him at the doorway. Smiled but with reserve. They walked through the house, her ahead of him in a fitted woollen dress and high-heeled shoes.

'This where I would like to have the conservatory,' she'd said.

She'd offered him coffee. He learned of their four children. He told her about his daughters.

She sat opposite him, composed and contained.

He glanced at her crossed leg that swung restlessly, her shapely carves, her neat ankles, her arched feet.

She saw his jawline, his broad shoulders, his long strong leanness.

They watched each other.

The inclination of his head.

Her small soft expressive hands.

His clean smile.

The upturned corners of her mouth.

He said that he would call again, to see how the work was progressing.

She told him that, of course, he was always welcome.

She stood at the open door as he went down the driveway.

He was aware that she was standing there.

Their hearts were pounding.

He made a time to call again. Said he wanted to inspect the work. When he got there, the maid told him that she was out.

He cast an impatient and cursory glance at the glass building. Did not notice the orchids. It was her that he'd hoped to see.

She phoned and apologised. One of her children needed to go to the dentist. Thank goodness she'd managed to get an appointment. She was sorry that she wasn't there when he came. She had a few things she wanted to show him in the conservatory. Would he be able to come by at some time?

The days were warm. Dew shimmered. Bees were busy. Buds were bursting.

Carla was dressed in silk, long and flowing, her hair in soft curls that nestled prettily into her neck. Her dark eyes shone, her face softly suffused with a rosy glow.

She was delighted with the conservatory, she told him, her voice husky, but there were a few small things that needed attending. 'Very small, but,' she laughed, 'you know me. A stickler for detail.'

'Oh sure, I do know you.' He laughed with her. 'Don't worry. I'll send our guys along.' He refused her offer of tea or coffee. Said that he had an appointment and needed to go.

She thanked him and took his hand at the front door. 'You've done a great job, Steve,' she breathed. 'I'm really happy with it.'

Her perfume stayed with him as he walked away. He felt stimulated. Somewhat out of control.

He resolved not to go back. 'Not a good idea,' he said aloud. He'd send the foreman for the sign-off.

But he could not get her out of his mind. He had to see her again.

The maid said that madam was at the pool. He walked through the house and down the steps to the terrace. On the water, sunbeams broke into shimmering sapphires. Against white walls, bougainvillea bunched lusciously in cerise and ochre. Above, the sky was a spread of unblemished blue.

Carla lay on a chaise longue, her head on her folded arms, her eyes closed, her body bare except for a tiny bikini.

Steve stood silently, watching her. His eyes travelled down her back, her legs, and back to her face. She gave no indication that she was aware of him.

'Carla,' he said.

Sleepily, she opened her eyes. 'Steve?' she smiled a slow smile. 'I wasn't expecting you.'

'We're signing off today. Did you forget?'

'No. I knew it was today. I thought we said later.'

'We said ten o'clock. It's ten now, exactly.' He looked at his watch. 'Ten. *Op die kop*. On the dot.'

'OK. No problem. We can do it now.' She sat up, stretched her arms above her head, smiled and, bare-breasted, shrugged into a sheer white shirt. 'Sorry you've caught me in a state of undress. I got used to sunbathing topless on the continent.' Her body showed through the flimsy garment. 'I hope I'm not embarrassing you.' She laughed and slipped her small feet into high-heeled mules.

Steve averted his gaze. 'Nothing I haven't seen before,' he laughed.

'That's right. You have seen all this before.' Her gaze was candid.

She turned and walked ahead of him. He watched the sway of her hips as she moved up the stairs and into the conservatory.

Among the orchids.

'My hobby,' she smiled, indicating the different varieties.

Boat orchids, lady slipper, vandas, hanging baskets with small delicate blooms in pinks and mauves, others with the markings of the tiger. There were those that looked like huge insects, others that had faces. Purples with bright yellow decorations. Others tall and elegant, immaculately white and pure as virgins.

'Gee. You've got quite a show here.' Steve walked around, admiring.

She touched a flower delicately with her small hand. 'I know. They're beautiful. My favourite flowers.'

'They're stunning,' he said. 'And doing well, by the looks of it.'

'Yes. The conservatory is working really well. Just the right amount of light and warmth. As you can see, they're flourishing.' She trailed a finger slowly along a stem, looking up at him, smiling.

The sun poured through the glass ceiling, holding them in a blaze of light.

'Well.' She became practical. 'Shall we get down to business? I need to sign off, don't I? And give you a cheque?'

'That's right.' He watched the light play on her flushed face, the lustre of her lips and her pearly teeth.

'Let's go into the study.' Her eyes smiled.

She swayed from the conservatory, ample in her transparent shirt. There was suggestion in her movements. This was the Carla he knew. A woman who used her body to send signals.

The study was dark and cool. Lined with books and leather couches.

She walked to the desk and picked up the contract. Then, sitting with straight back and rounded thighs suggestively splayed on either side of an upholstered armchair, she glanced impatiently at the pages. 'I never read these things,' she sighed. 'They're so boring. I take it that everything's in order. That all I need to do is sign?'

'You should read before you sign.'

They were speaking of the contract but their eyes and minds were on each other.

She looked away. 'Oh! There it is.' Her laugh tinkled. 'My bikini top.'

She held it up then slipped off her shirt and covered her nipples with the tiny triangles of material. She turned her naked back to him. 'Will you tie this for me?'

He took the thin cords from her hands, his fingers fumbling against her skin. She was silky and smooth under his touch.

The room began to throb.

'Carla,' he said softly. You don't really want to put this on, do you?'

She turned her eyes to his. 'How do you mean, Steve?' Her voice was husky.

'I mean that you don't want to put this on. You want it off. You want me to see you without it. Don't you?'

'Do you want to see me without it?' Her voice teased.

He threw the top aside and slipped his arms around her. 'Carla.' He breathed in her perfume.

'Steve.' Her heart raced. Her hands entangled in his hair. Gently she pushed him away. 'We shouldn't,' she whispered.

He pulled her towards him and, with vehemence, kissed her.

Urgently, their eyes burning, they clung to each other, their desire mounting, becoming insatiable.

She whispered his name with love, with longing. 'Steve. Oh Steve. I've waited such a long time for you.'

Her eyes were wet with tears. Gently he wiped them away.

They came together.

Again and again.

Wave after passionate wave in the dimness of that room.

Until finally, replete and exhausted, they fell apart.

Steve drove away from her house dazed. Carla and him? How on earth that had happened?

He knew she'd set the scene. But I was up for it, he told himself. He'd wanted her as much as she did him.

'What a woman.' He became stimulated just thinking about her. Her mouth, breasts, her thighs, the way she moved, the way she used her hands…

'Hey! Pull yourself together!' he said, allowing himself to laugh. 'It was fun. But that's it.'

Only then did he think of Laura. 'For God's sake! What am I thinking? I'm married. She's married. This is crazy.'

She phoned him that afternoon at his office. When he heard her voice, he excused himself from his meeting to take the call.

'Steve,' she said. Her voice was yielding. 'I forgot to give you the cheque. And the contract. We never completed the contract.'

'I know,' he smiled into the phone. 'I'll get it from you.'

Then, almost in a whisper, 'It was good. Wasn't it? Steve?'

'It was more than good.' His voice was gruff. 'It was great. Really. Great.'

He told himself that this was crazy. It had to stop. But he found it difficult to keep away from her. In fact, impossible.

She was there to please him. She intrigued him. Stimulated him in ways unknown to him. In some ways distasteful, but, being Carla, with her dark eyes, her moist mouth and feverish hands, she managed to get away with it.

It was as though they were young again, full of the intensity and fire of youth.

They could not keep away from each other. Steve left meetings and cut business acquaintances short when Carla's calls came, calls to say that the coast was clear, that the maid was out of the house, that they could be together.

He parked in a lane behind the house and entered through the back door. At first, this deception perturbed him. Steve had never previously found a need to hide from anyone or anything. All his dealings were upfront and straight forward.

But this was different. The arousal he experienced whilst being with Carla overruled all else.

He waited with impatience for the moment she would open the door, for her smile, for her soft hands that reached out to him, for the intoxication of her perfume. The subtle promises of her body overwhelmed him.

And so Steve, who had never entered a back door in his life, slipped in through the servants' entrance and into her arms.

There were times that they would devour each other in the passage-way.

There were times, when the maid was off for the afternoon, they would leisurely indulge in their lovemaking for a few hours, and then cling longingly to each other at the door.

When Ian had a conference, and their sons were at camp, when their daughter was asleep, Carla and Steve managed to spend a whole evening in the marital bed. She told him how she prayed every night that they would be able to spend all their nights together. He heard her words. He chose not to answer her.

On another hot evening, they swam together and made love in the pool, breaking the smooth reflection of moonlight on the water into ripples.

The maid watched them from behind a wall.

But most of their time together needed to be stolen. An hour in the study, on the lounge settee, in the bedroom, on the stairs, and even among the orchids.

She told him over and over again how much she loved him.

He told Laura he would be late in coming home. He had important things to attend to. In his mind, this answer was not a lie. He was attending to things. Important things. That's what he told himself.

He felt alive and happy. He would come home stimulated, buoyant and strangely excited. He tried to convince himself that, in that state, he would be better company for Laura.

But he needed to be careful. His car was distinctive. He parked in a small lane behind Carla's house, under a thick canopy of trees. The only thing was the 'fucking birdshit'. Every time he parked there, the car was covered in it.

Laura came home one afternoon and saw the gardener hosing down the stairs. It happened again.

'Where are you parking?' she asked. 'Your car's such a mess.'

The maid knocked on the door. Laura was irritated. She'd told them not to disturb her if the door was closed, except to bring in the tea at eleven o'clock.

'Ma'am. There's someone wants to see you. A man…'

Looming behind her large frame, and now pushing past her without waiting for a response, was the tall figure of Ian. His face was dark, his expression hostile.

'Hello.' He nodded at Laura. 'Sorry to barge in on you like this.'

She looked up at him, perplexed. 'What is it? Why are you here?'

'I've got something to tell you. Something to show you.' His voice was strained.

'Please,' she said, 'sit down. Would you like some tea?'

He remained standing, unbending, his eyes burning like fiery coals. 'I don't want anything. I'll come straight to the point.'

Alarmed by the intensity of his gaze, she pushed away from her desk, warily watching him. His mouth was a thin line, his expression strange.

'What is it? What's the matter?'

'They're having an affair.'

'Who?'

'Steve and Carla.'

'What!'

Ian did not respond. It was as though he, too, was not able to process what he'd just said. The room was heavy with silence. She heard him suck in the air.

'What did you say?' Laura asked, her voice low.

'You heard me,' he barked. 'Your husband and my wife. They're having an affair.'

'How do you know?'

'I'll tell you how I know. Someone saw his car parked behind the house. Someone else saw him coming and going in the middle of the day. I asked Carla. She said he'd come to look at the job. But the job was finished. We'd paid him.' Pain crossed his face. Distraught, he pushed his hand through his hair.

She waited, her heart pounding, her hands forming tight fists.

'I began to watch her. She seemed different. I came home one day and heard her laughing on the phone. When she saw me, she got a fright. Put the phone down without saying goodbye. I could sense she was up to something. I tried to ignore it. Didn't want to doubt her. Carla. My wife.' He brushed his hand across his eyes.

'I've had someone watch them. A private detective.' He shook his head. 'Can you believe it? I've been paying a guy to spy on them. A professional. With surveillance. Cameras. Our phone's been tapped. The whole toot… It's all here. Photographs. Recorded conversations…'

She stared at the thick envelope he passed to her.

His voice broke. Anguished, he urged her to open it. 'Go ahead. Have a look. See what your swine of a husband's been up to with my beautiful bitch of a wife.'

Laura stared at him, uncomprehending.

'Go on. Look. You're in for a shock. A real big shock.'

She glanced at the envelope.

He turned away, his tall figure moving towards the door. 'I'm leaving. There's nothing more to say.' He motioned to the package. 'Those are yours,' he said. Then, 'Don't forget to listen to the phone calls. They're a real treat.'

Laura stared at the envelope on her desk. Light drained from the room. Images blurred. The air was a fog. A dullness crept into her mind and a cold numbness seeped through her body. There were sounds she that could not hear, a scent from roses that she could not smell.

She was transfixed. Could not tear her gaze from it. It was ugly. Threatening and frightening.

She remained unmoving until, from what seemed far away, she heard the phone ring. Automatically she reached for it.

It was his voice. He sounded buoyant. He told her that her birthday coming up and that he wanted to celebrate with her 'starting right now!' He would take her for an early dinner to Saverrilli's. Her favourite restaurant. He'd booked for a live show afterwards. He was not going to tell her what show. It was going to be a surprise. A big surprise. He knew that she would love it.

Automatically she replied, 'OK' to his 'See you soon.'

All the time, the envelope stared balefully at her. Challenging her to pick it up, to open it. She could not.

When she heard Steve's voice, his footsteps down the passage, without knowing why, she hid the envelope between the pages of a book.

He burst into the study, exuberant, happy, smiling broadly. 'Hi, sweetheart,' his voice rang out as he bent to kiss her. 'For you!' he beamed, presenting her with a massive bouquet of bright and beautiful blooms. 'For the birthday girl! My special girl! A couple of days early but I couldn't wait.'

She took the flowers and laid them on the desk. She looked at him. Her face was pale, her eyes dull.

Concerned, he asked, 'Laura. Sweetheart. What is it? You don't look yourself.'

'I had a visitor today.' Her voice was flat, her expression wooden.

'Who?'

'Ian. Carla's husband.'

'Ian? What did he want?' He was instantly alert.

She turned to face him, her voice fading. 'He came to tell me that you and Carla were having an affair.'

'He said what!'

'That you and Carla were having an affair.'

Steve felt panic rise within him. 'An affair?' he repeated in a shocked tone. 'Me? With Carla?'

'That's what he said.'

'Is he crazy?' To mask his fright, his response was angry. 'Carla and me? The guy's out of his mind. Where on earth did he get that from?'

'That's what he said, Steve. That's what he came to tell me.'

'Is that what he said! Well! God knows where that comes from! A load of bullshit! Absolute rubbish! I'll go and see him. I'll go there right now and I'll ask him what the hell he's talking about. What on earth would I want with Carla? The guy's lost it. He's out of his mind.'

He drove down the driveway. Perspiration drenched the back of his shirt. His hands were damp with sweat. Filled with trepidation, he compelled himself to think straight. Somehow or other, he needed to talk his way out of this. Deny it.

He'll deny it. He'll ask Ian where he got this from, tell him it was a load of hogwash. That all he ever did in their home was to examine the work and have their contract signed off.

He wondered if Carla had said anything. He did not think she would. He'd made it clear to her that their liaison was over. He told her that he would not leave Laura. They both needed to get back to their former lives. She'd accepted that. She cried. Sure, she cried. But she accepted it.

He told her that she would not have wanted to antagonise Ian. She had a good life with him and not to forget their four children. She needed to consider them.

No, he thought, she would not have said anything.

He told himself that he needed to get through this inconvenience with as little fuss and bother as possible.

He'd transgressed. That was true. But the whole thing was insignificant, a little blot that had occurred, that would dissipate, that, in his mind, had all but disappeared. He needed to get his marriage back on track.

Laura… She was everything to him. She was the love of his life. The most beautiful person he knew. His wife. The mother of his children. He must not lose her.

He needed to handle this carefully. Make it right. Make it go away.

He felt anxious as he rang the doorbell. He knew that Ian was a clever, measured man who weighed his words carefully. He would not have acted on impulse. This was going to be a challenge, but all he needed was to stick to his guns.

He was sure that no one had ever actually seen him coming and going from their house. The maid was always out when he was there. As far as he was concerned, there was nothing to incriminate them.

In any event, it hadn't been a big deal. At worst an insignificant little flirtation. That's all he would admit to, if pushed.

Ian opened the door. His eyes were like stones. He stared rigidly at Steve.

'Hi.' Steve met his gaze without flinching.

'What do you want?' Ian's voice was tight and angry.

'I want an explanation.' Steve tried to match Ian's aggression.

'An explanation?' Ian sneered. 'What's there to explain?'

'You came to my house today. You told my wife some cock 'n' bull story about Carla and me.'

'Cock 'n' bull, is it?'

Behind him, Carla hovered anxiously, her hands on her pale face. She did not look at him.

'Of course it is! You know that.'

Ian remained silent.

'All I ever did here was to manage your job,' Steve blustered. 'To see that everything was properly done. I had no other reason to be here.'

'You came here to manage the job?' Ian smirked. 'You had no other reason to be here?'

'That's right. And once it was done, we signed off.'

Ian's eyes were now sharply focused. 'Did Laura show you the photographs I gave her?'

'Photographs? What photographs? What are you talking about?' Steve stammered.

'Did she play you the recordings of your telephone conversations?'

'Recordings?'

'Go home. Ask your wife to show you the stuff I gave her. It's all there. In black and white. Go home. Have a look. Have a listen. Carla's seen them. She's heard them. We listened to them together. Didn't we, my darling wife?'

He turned to Carla. She shrank away from him.

Ian stared at Steve. 'Do you know what you are?' he said venomously. 'You're a piece of crap.' He pointed to Carla. 'So is she. My hot little wife… Both of you. Real crap.'

The door closed in his face.

Steve stood still. He was stunned.

Ian said that there were photographs. There were recordings of his telephone conversations. All those things they'd said to each other over the phone. Her tinkling laugh, her blowing of kisses, her whispered words that caused him to bulge uncomfortably in his pants. What he'd promised to do to her. How she'd begged, 'Stop it, Steve. You're making me come.' All those dirty words.

Oh God! Surely that was not recorded? What if Laura had heard all that? Sweat ran down his back and beaded thickly on his forehead.

He needed to get back to his wife. As quickly as possible.

Then he recalled that she'd not mentioned seeing or hearing any of the so-called evidence. Perhaps she'd chosen not to look. Not to listen.

Perhaps she'll throw it into a bin and say, 'Steve, if something happened between you and Carla, I don't want to know about it. Our life together is more important than Carla,' and he would take her in his arms and reassure her. Tell her how right she was. How much he loved her.

Perhaps that's what would happen…

He drove back in the dusk. Clouds banked heavily. Trees blanched and were ghostly. His heart drummed loudly and forcefully in his chest. His eyes burned and his mouth felt parched.

Please, he said to himself. Please let her understand. Let her see this for what it is. A crazy moment of madness in the context of a whole lifetime. An insignificant nothing that that's come and gone. Something that means nothing to me. Absolutely nothing. Just a crazy moment of madness.

Laura, his mind cried, I'm sorry. So sorry. I did wrong. I should never have done this. Please. Please. My darling. Forgive me.

Laura, who was terrified of electric storms, stood at the terrace door, unaware of the piercing blades of blinding white light that slashed the ominous clouds, not registering the terrifying claps of thunder.

She stood as still as stone. Her eyes were fixed to the splay of photographs on the desk. She'd torn open the envelope, looked at the first few photos, then thrown them down in disbelief and horror.

She'd felt the blood drain from her face, from her being, leaving her as cold as ice. She struggled to breathe. She, who would close curtains and draw blinds against storms, who had hidden under beds in fear of them when she was a child, who cowered behind her mother and buried her head in her mother's skirt, now opened the glass door wide and desperately sucked in the storm's air, struggling not to fall, not to give in to her body that did not want to support her.

She became rigid, her eyes wide in her white face, her body outlined by vicious gashes of light. So shocked was she, so void of any feeling, that she felt as though life itself was leaving her.

It was in this state that Steve found her. In the gloom, her back lashed by pellets of rain.

'Laura!' he cried. 'Laura, come away from the window.'

She turned to him, her eyes filled with excruciating pain. She saw him without knowing him, staring uncomprehendingly as though he was a stranger.

Then, from some place deep within her came an anguished cry that filled the room, reaching into every corner – a sound that was not human, that rent him to shreds.

'Oh, Steve. What have you done…'

Those words would haunt him for the rest of his life.

She'd left him there, had slipped away, an unseeing shadow, from the shadows in the room.

Her cry, like that of a tortured animal, echoed in his mind. Agitated, he ran up the stairs to the first floor. She was not in their bedroom. He ran down the passage to Arielle's room.

He looked at her helplessly, at her hollow eyes, at her twisting hands. 'Laura…' he whispered.

She did not seem to see him or hear him, turning away when he offered her water.

'Do you want me to call the doctor?' he asked, his voice ravaged.

That was all he could think of – a doctor… Perhaps a doctor could help…

In the early dawn hours, Laura fell into an uneasy doze hugging Arielle's pillow. She awoke to a grey day with the wind howling through the garden, tearing at bushes and trees.

Sitting up in bed, momentarily confused, she shivered uncontrollably in the cold pale light as she recalled the horrors of the previous evening.

She remembered how, in her terrible state, she'd gone down the dark stairs and along the dark passages determined to retrieve the incriminating contents in the envelope.

Filled with a sense of dread, she reached for her handbag. It was there.

Taking small unsteady steps, she walked to Arielle's bathroom, stepped into the shower and held onto the bar, letting the water run over her.

She looked into the mirror. Her pale reflection watched her.

'Focus,' she said aloud. 'For God's sake. Think.'

She told herself that she needed to see an attorney. Right away.

There was only one person she could think of. Manfred. She would insist on an appointment immediately. He had to see her. Today.

She also had to get as far from Steve as she could. Move out of this dreadful house. As soon as possible. Today if possible.

She dried her hair, dressed, smudged colour onto her pale lips, and made the phone call.

He would see her within the hour.

She arrived too early for the appointment.

'Perhaps you'd like to go for a coffee and come back in a little while,' his secretary suggested.

In the café, she ordered tea and toast, gulping down the hot liquid, ignoring the toast.

Manfred took her hand. 'Laura,' he said warmly, kissing her cheek. 'Come on in.' He was his genial self in his crumpled suit, his jowls folding comfortably over his collar.

She remembered Steve's assessment of him. That his casual approach concealed an acute and calculating mind. 'He's one of the sharpest guys in the business,' he'd told her.

She had no words. She handed him the envelope, her eyes averted, flickering without registering to the certificates on the wall. She would not look at the contents that were now spread before him, would not look at those images again.

There followed an oppressive silence. A grey day infiltrated the office space.

Manfred, practised in self-control, always in charge of his emotions, was, for once, lost for words. 'Good God!' was his comment as he pushed himself away from his desk. He watched her tense face, saw her twisted hands.

He took a deep breath then blew the air out in a soft whistle. 'I can only guess why you've come to me. But you must realise that I can't handle this.'

'I came to you because I didn't know where else to go,' she pleaded. 'I need your help.'

'Laura, I'm his lawyer.'

'I need advice.'

'What advice are you looking for?' Manfred's voice became clinical.

'I want a divorce. I can't stay with him now. After this…' She glanced at the photographs. 'I can't stay with him.' Her eyes appealed to him. 'Surely you can see that?'

Manfred fingered his jowls. 'I don't do divorces, Laura.' His words were measured.

'OK. But if you can't help me, you need to tell me where to go, who I should see.' Her voice became insistent. 'You need to give me the name of a divorce lawyer. That's not difficult for you, is it?'

'This is all difficult for me. Steve's my lifelong friend. I'm his legal advisor. You're my friend. I really wish you hadn't come to me. You're putting me in a very difficult position.' He paused, then packed the photographs into the envelope and handed them to her. 'Look, Laura, this is a legal centre. The whole building's full of lawyers. Why don't you go down and look on the board?'

'The board? Is that the best you can do?'

He looked at his watch, a heavy gold face on a thick gold chain band, and said firmly, 'I'm afraid so… Look, I'm really sorry. I really can't say more. You'll have to excuse me.' He ushered her from his office, his hand lightly on her back, his face creased into a weak smile.

Then, behind a closed door, he sank heavily into his chair. 'Jeez!' he exclaimed to himself. 'What a stink!'

Letting out a soft whistle he ran his hands over his thinning hair. Steve! Good God! What on earth had possessed him?

The days that followed were tumultuous. Steve resolved to do everything to repair the damage, to use his all experience and abilities to negotiate an outcome that would ameliorate the disaster that faced him.

He decided that he would tell Laura whatever she wanted to know. She was an honest and straightforward person. She would appreciate straight talk from him. That's the way to go with her. To get through to her.

He tried. God, how he tried.

She walked away without giving him any indication of whether she'd heard him.

He confessed to his daughters. It was extremely difficult for him to tell them that he'd been having sex with someone other than their mother. He tried to minimise it, referring to his 'unfortunate little dalliance'.

'What's that, Dad?' Arielle asked bluntly.

'A mistake,' he replied. 'I made a mistake.'

She told the girls that the marriage was over. That she wanted a divorce. 'Oh God, Ma,' cried Arielle. 'Do you want me to come?'

'No,' Laura answered. 'You don't have to do that. I'm OK. I'm seeing a lawyer. He'll put everything in place. It'll take time. I'm going to move out of the house. I've already spoken to an agent. I've asked her to find me a flat. She'll let me know as soon as she has something suitable. In the meantime, I'm going to stay with Granny.' Her voice was quiet and controlled.

'You sound so calm, Ma, so together… Are you sure you're OK?'

'I'm fine. I've got a lot to see to, a lot to sort out, but I'll be fine. Don't worry. I'm OK.'

Carolyn asked her what had happened. Why she thought Steve had done this? They'd always thought the marriage was solid. They seemed a really together couple. 'What happened to cause Dad to have an affair?'

Laura was sure that her older daughter was looking to blame her for her father's infidelity. It would give Carolyn reason to excuse him. She'd always favoured her dad.

'After all, men need – you know – sex. That's how men are. And women need to meet their desires. To come up to the mark. To be appealing,' said Carolyn.

Laura would not allow herself to progress this discussion. Calmly she replied that she was unaware of any reason for Steve to have done what he did. As far as she was concerned, their marriage was as it had always been. Except, she admitted to herself, during the last few months when he'd changed.

Perhaps Carolyn was right. Perhaps she'd not done sufficient to keep Steve interested. Perhaps he'd strayed because he no longer found her attractive.

The porcelain statue. Elongated. Futuristic. A tall slim portrayal of a woman standing on the balls of her feet, her long thin arms and slender fingers stretching, reaching above her. Her head was thrown back, her hair fell sleekly, her robe clung to her breasts and thighs.

Steve had given it to Laura as a wedding gift. He thought she was beautiful. Graceful. Elegant. Enigmatic.

She stood on the half-moon marble-topped hall table, her image reflected in a gilt mirror.

'What do you think she's doing?' Laura asked him.

'I think she's reaching for the stars.'

'And you?' she asked her mother.

'I think she's praying to God.'

She turned to her father. 'Dad?'

'To me, she looks like she's reaching for a suitcase.' He laughed his gruff laugh. 'I think she's leaving.'

When Carolyn was a small girl, she meticulously washed an empty jam jar, scraped off the label, filled it with water and placed five pristine white daisies. Reaching on tiptoe, she carefully put the improvised little vase next to the statue. 'Those flowers are our family,' she'd said solemnly.

'But there are five flowers and we are only four.'

'One is for Daddy, one is for Mommy, one is for Arielle and one is for me.'

'And the fifth?'

The child had shyly smiled, 'That one is for love.'

The statue of the woman stood on the table for all the years, its blurred features indicating neither joy nor sorrow, its elegance no longer noticed, its interpretation no longer of interest. The maid wiped it down each week and placed it precisely in the same position, a mirror image behind it.

On the day that Laura left, the statue was no longer on the

half-moon table. It lay scattered in many porcelain pieces on the cold tiles in the empty hall of the house.

She was gone.

He walked down the lifeless expanse of corridors and into the vast rooms, the rooms she chose not to go into, the rooms she did care for. The rooms that she did not decorate.

'Go with my mother,' he'd suggested. 'She knows what to buy. She's got good taste. An eye for paintings. Knows about antiques. Go with her. She'll help you to make the right choices.'

Laura tried. They walked in and out of furniture shops, upholstery stores, antique dealers, art dealers.

She stared at the paintings, heard the names of the artists, looked at antiques uncomprehendingly, not understanding the differences between English and French pieces, heard her mother-in-law advise, 'Go for the French. French is better.'

Exhausted, she traipsed around, in and out, up and down, until finally, and carefully choosing her words, she said to Steve's mother, 'You're so good at this. I'm totally ignorant. I'm confused with the colours. All those fabrics. I don't know what to choose. And as far as the antiques are concerned, to be honest, I don't know anything about antiques. I don't want to choose something Steve won't like. Same with the paintings. I don't know the artists.

'I'm finding all this really difficult. What I'd like to say is, and I really hope you don't mind, but do you think we could leave the decorating to you? I would appreciate it, and I know that Steve will as well. He says you know so much. If you could do the decorating for us, that would be fantastic...'

His mother listened and quietly nodded, taking care not to show how delighted she was at this prospect. She'd found shopping with Laura tedious and frustrating. Because she was mindful not to impose her own taste on her, she'd taken care to consult Laura on every detail.

Laura really did not know a thing about decorating, she'd confided to her sister, 'She has absolutely no idea. Not a clue. Never grew up with it. So she's asked me to do the house for them,' she sighed. As though it was a burden for her.

Then, thrilled and elated, she embarked on her mission with energy and enthusiasm, giving full vent to her talent for decorating, and even greater vent to her talent for spending vast sums of money.

She chose blue silk for the formal lounge, creating what she fondly referred to as the Blue Room – azure for chaise longues and sofas, and carefully selected bureaus, a huge armoire, a console, marquetry tables, a few lamps…

Also, the sculpture of horses, the carving of the face of an old man.

'Such character,' she breathed.

Showing visitors around, proudly, with a sense of ownership, as though it was her house, she pointed to her favourite artists hanging on the ivory walls, and the marble statue in the entrance hall…

She would have liked to have got rid of the elongated woman with the upstretched arms on the half-moon table, but Steve told her, 'Don't touch that.'

He walked into the Blue Room – the faded blue velvet drapes trimmed with fringes and held back with sashes, the huge marble fireplace, the cold brocades and glowing silks in the formal lounge that was hardly used.

He opened the interleading doors to the dining room, a space that he declared could seat twenty guests comfortably. The massive table with its matching antique epergnes and heavy silver candlesticks. The crystal chandelier, the crystal wine decanters. The matching velvet drapes.

'Important,' he remembered his mother smilingly explaining, 'When the doors are open between the lounge and the dining room, there must always be a flow of colour and fabric.'

Bevelled glass doors opened to the terrace. He wandered out into the garden. There were no stars. The moon was distorted behind dense cloud. Heavy air predicted a storm. The plants were sombre, the trees spectral against the dark sky.

The calm before the storm, he thought. Ominous and overbearing, it predicted uncontrollable forces that would rage, ensuing damage and irredeemable destruction.

He sat on the steps in the face of it.

For a moment, the moon broke out of the clouds and the garden lighted up in black and white. The immaculate driveway, the ordered borders, the grouped shrubs, the trees strategically placed.

Just the right amount of shade in all the right places.

'I want a smart garden,' he'd told her as she stared at the line of gardeners. 'Not a jumbled mess like the last one…'

He remembered how sad she was to leave their first house, where their two small girls dressed like fairies and waved their wands among sweet-smelling shrubs and pungent herbs, between rose bushes and carnations and dahlias and tomatoes that grew haphazardly and in profusion. The lemon tree, and the scent of almonds, and blossoms that fell like confetti on the children, who giggled and declared that they were brides. Or took their dolls for walks through higgledy piggledy paths and had picnics on sunny patches of lawn.

She'd described that garden in her stories, a magical place her children believed to be a home for elves and fairies.

Now the girls were gone.

Laura was gone.

Trixie had refused to move in. Never gave the new house a chance.

He remembered the day as though it was yesterday. The children waiting at the creaking gate, swinging on it. They screamed with excitement when he drove into the driveway and danced around him, their faces pink with excitement.

'What?' he'd laughed.

'We won a dog!' Carolyn yelled. 'We won a dog on *Pet's Parade*!'

'We dialled the number and we won a dog! They said our names on the radio! That we won a dog!' chimed Arielle ecstatically.

'They did,' confirmed Laura, beaming. 'They finally got through. They've been trying so hard. Every Saturday. Today they got through. We're getting a dog.'

They had to wait until Monday. Until they got back from school. Rushed up the path bursting with excitement and anticipation.

The dog was not as described in the program. They expected a fox terrier puppy. What arrived was an older animal that might have had some terrier in its genes. Steve estimated it to be at least eight years old. That dog, he'd said, had seen decidedly better years.

None of this perturbed the children. They were delighted with their win.

The dog showed them how he could beg for food. He shook hands by offering a paw. He rolled over. He got onto hind legs and danced when there was music.

He'd learned all this from previous owners. He'd had many owners, too many to remember. But he did recall the owner who made him dance on hind legs for the duration of a 78 on a turntable. How he was made to move around on his hind legs for fear of that whip that was used on him. How the friends would laugh and say, 'Pete, put on another record. Make him do it again…' The dog remembered that owner and those lessons. As soon as there was music, he automatically danced on hind legs.

Steve thought the dog very clever. All the tricks he could do. 'We'll call him Trixie. That's a good name for him,' he laughed.

Trixie'd had as many names as he'd had owners. Names meant nothing to him. He'd once had the esteemed name of Frederick, given by a man with flowing white hair who wore a silk dressing gown and used perfume. The food there was quite good but the dog could not take to the owner, and so, as he had done many times in the past, he upped and left.

Of course he would end up in the pound again, but he did not mind. Unlike the other dogs, he felt safe on concrete behind wire fences. He waited. Sooner or later, there would be another person scrutinising him, looking into his soulful eyes, and off he would go to yet another home – for as long as it suited him.

The new place wasn't bad. The small girls were sweet and gentle. The man and the woman were kind. It did not mean that he was becoming attached to them. He'd stopped attaching himself many owners ago. But it was OK. It would do for the meantime.

He was beginning to feel quite comfortable when the upheaval took place. The move to the new house. They took him there get him used to 'a different environment'.

Trixie walked among the mounds of black earth mixed with smelly compost that were being dug into the ground to serve the new plants for the carefully planned garden. He sniffed his way around and thought about this place. He decided that it would not serve him well. There were too many strange people here, gardeners who might kick him when no one was around, maids who may beat him with a stick as had happened in a previous life.

No, he thought. This will not work for me. He knew that he needed to get away.

While they were distracted, he quietly slipped out of the gate and with his chopped tail erect, marched determinedly down the street. He was soon out of sight.

Steve remembered how devastated Laura and the children were. He, too, was upset. He'd grown fond of the old dog.

He recalled how they'd searched. Up and down the streets. Knocking on doors. Asking the neighbours. Reporting their loss to the SPCA. Going back to the pound.

For months, they searched. For years, they looked out for Trixie.

But they never found him and Trixie never came back.

Steve wondered where the photographs were. He'd left them on the desk. He opened the drawers and scrambled among papers, but they were not there. Laura must have them, he thought woodenly.

If the photographs and the recordings had not existed, if Ian had not hired someone to spy on them, how different this would all have been. It would have just gone away.

He and Carla had planned for such an outcome on their last visit together as they calmly faced each other, each understanding that the affair was over.

Steve told her that he loved Laura. That he would never leave her. That she was everything to him. He said that what he and Carla had indulged in was lust, not love. That although they'd shared a great passion together, it was over. He would always respect her and have regard for her, but they now needed to put their relationship behind them, to go back to their previous lives. This was what he wanted. He was sure that she would want the same.

She'd listened. Her mouth drooped. She'd answered that yes, she heard what he said, and yes, in a logical way and in a perfect world, they could put it to bed (she'd smiled at that, or not smiled, he wasn't sure). But, she continued, the great difficulty for her was that she was in love with him, had always been and would be until the day she died. She thought that they could somehow be together. Get divorced and marry each other. She'd looked at him with dark eyes and reached for his hand.

He moved away from her touch. She cried.

'It's not going to happen, Carla. You must get that out of your mind. My life is with Laura. She's the woman I married, she's the mother of our girls. She's the love of my life.' He was brutal. 'I chose her over you because I fell in love with her. That will never change.'

She sobbed.

Gently he said, 'Carla, listen to me. You have a good man in Ian. A great guy who worships you. You have four kids. A grandchild on the way. You and Ian have built a whole life together. Go back to him and love him in the way he deserves. Move away from this. Move on.'

Then he did take her hand, appealing to her better senses. 'We need to be sensible, Carla. We have to handle this right. If we do it right, no one need be hurt.'

He'd turned her face to his. 'Look at me, Carla. Listen to what I'm saying. 'We don't want to hurt them, do we?'

He looked around the small room. Laura's refuge. The couch that she curled into. The desk where she wrote. The only room in the house that she liked.

This was the room where she spent her time. There were evenings when he would come home early to find her earnestly bent over her work, her hair tied back, her face devoid of make-up. Sometimes he thought her plain and even unattractive in her cotton shirt and baggy pants. She'd be deep in thought, contemplating the right choice of word or phrase, and, irritated, he would walk away.

He was vaguely aware that her writing skills were developing. She'd had several short stories published, had won prizes in two competitions, was honing a novel. He recalled that she was frustrated with it because it was not conveying what she meant. He'd been casual in his response. Why, he asked himself, did he not show more interest? Because he did not think of her as a writer. Did not give her work much credit. As far as he was concerned, writing was her hobby, a mere pastime.

She'd tried to tell him about the stories she wrote for children in the cancer ward at the hospital. Each week, she spent two mornings reading her stories to the patients. She personalised them, using the children's names and the names of their brothers or sisters, and their pets, their dogs or cats or rabbits or birds. Arielle had illustrated the little books. All her images had smiling faces that caused the children to smile and sometimes laugh. She'd described how heartbroken parents would meet her in the passages and tell her that they would keep the little book she'd written for their child. They would keep it forever.

A waste of time, he thought. But it was doing no harm. It kept her occupied.

He'd answered, 'God. I don't know how you do it. So depressing.'

There was nothing more for her to say. 'He doesn't understand,' she told herself. And, 'He's really not interested.'

After a while, she simply answered his question, 'What did you do today?' with 'Oh. The usual. I took the kids to dancing, to their speech lessons, their Spanish dancing, and ballet.' Laura smilingly confided to him that neither of them would ever become ballerinas.

But, he remembered, there was another side to his wife, a confident sophisticated side. Always the excellent hostess, she welcomed guests to her home with a radiant warmth, into rooms filled with flowers, to a table she'd set with simple but undeniable chic. She was charming, gracious and attentive in a refined and unobtrusive way.

'When she needs to, she comes up to the mark,' her father-in-law said quietly and with admiration.

'Yes,' his wife grudgingly agreed. 'Pity she doesn't do it more often.'

Steve was delighted with these impressions. It was important to him that she was noticed and admired. He never asked himself why it was that he needed accolades and compliments for his wife. But, gratified, he would kiss her and tell her that he always knew that she had it in her. That, if she tried, she could really carry it off.

She answered that she did not know what he was on about. What was there to having people to dinner? What was the big deal? Why was it so important to him?

Why had it been so important? he now wondered. Why had he needed to feel proud of her, to show her off, to convey a lifestyle of extravagance and indulgence. Why was this what he needed? Why was this all that he understood?

There were times that he'd found her lacking. She did not seem to understand his life, or take advantage of his success. She was not tempted by opulence. Did not bother to wear the jewels he bought her. Would not have a new car every year. Dreaded leaving the girls when they went overseas.

She also did not realise that she was often derided her friends. She did not fit the mould. Nevertheless, they trusted her, confided in her and asked for her advice. They saw in Laura intelligence, a sharp perception, kindness and understanding.

She quietly observed that their indulgent lifestyle did nothing to alleviate their issues. Money did not solve their problems. She noted that they were often ill at ease beneath their sheaths of silk and lavish jewels.

She thought that they were misguided. Did not have the right values. They drifted from shop to shop, from hairdresser to manicurist.

They did not seem to have direction. They sought their fulfilment in the achievements of their children. They were never satisfied.

She told herself, you have to be grateful for what you have. You have to be your own person… You need to keep things as simple and uncomplicated as possible. That was her philosophy on life.

He'd thought that they'd grown apart.

He recalled how much she disliked the house, how she'd never wanted to be there. He'd worked with the architect, had told him that he wanted a house like his father's. His father had built their mansion after making his fortune. He was well on the way to making more money than his dad ever had, and he now needed all the trappings of a successful businessman.

He recalled how Laura was overwhelmed by the size of the rooms, the endless passages. How she'd disliked the majestic staircase with its handcrafted banister, its ornamental leaves and branches. How distressed she was to be removed from her girls, whose suite of rooms was on the other side of the landing.

How she'd walked through the huge fitted kitchen, opened a drawer, looked inside and closed it again. How he'd said, 'You don't have to know what's in here. The cook will take over. She'll see to everything. You, my darling, will be the lady of the house, just giving orders…'

How she'd looked at him bewildered, and how she'd had tears in her eyes.

All those empty rooms in that hollow house. As empty and hollow as the man who now walked through them.

He was motionless in the emptiness. In the meaningless spaces. He touched the banister of metal vine leaves that looked as though they, too, would shrivel and die.

Perfumes permeated from the rose garden of carefully chosen and nurtured blooms. Among them were his mother's pride and joy, 'Old roses, including tea roses,' she boasted proudly. A new cultivar named after some European queen had been imported by Steve. He did not know whether it would take in the southern hemisphere, but remembered giving his personal attention to the thorny little stem that, after a few disappointing seasons began to flourish with great beauty and abundance.

He shrugged. The garden. The roses. What does it mean?

Nothing.

From the kitchen came the loud chatter of the maids, those sullen overbearing women Laura could not control. When she'd complained to Steve, he told her to remember that she was the boss. She paid their wages. She was in charge. She'd looked at him despairingly, then walked way.

Standing in the hall, he now recognised her isolation in that house of many rooms, her uneasiness in its immensity, where the servants, noisily chatting in the kitchen, were more at home than she was.

Suddenly angry, he felt a need to assert his authority. 'Martha,' he yelled, 'come here.'

'Mastah?' She stood there, watching him.

How many times Laura had complained about her insolence, her lack of response, 'When I talk to her, she pretends not to hear me.' Not allowing Laura into the kitchen. Standing, implacable, immovable, her bulk protecting the space she took to be her domain.

Steve had ignored Laura's complaints. His standard response was, 'But she's a great cook. You can't complain about her food. If you could cook like her…'

He watched the woman. For a moment, he too sensed insubordination. 'Bring me some tea,' he ordered brusquely. 'And make it quick.'

He remembered Laura's quiet suggestion. Now that the girls were gone, perhaps they should move. All those empty rooms. She'd said it quickly, as though she was afraid he would stop her before she finished what she needed to say.

He recalled his silence. Then, 'Why would we want to do that, Laura?' His words were measured. 'The kids will come back. They'll come on holiday. They'll need somewhere to stay.'

'We could move into something smaller. Something more manageable. With a couple of spare bedrooms,' she'd answered desperately. 'We could still put them up. Still make them comfortable.'

'A couple of spare bedrooms? After all this? Your girls are spoilt. They're used to luxury. Their own suites. Come on, Laura. Don't be in such a hurry. Why move now? We can still enjoy this house for years to come.'

He found his way to the little lounge. To the place where he most strongly sensed her.

Laura at her desk. The sun striping into the room catching the red in her hair. Her delicate profile, the slanting light from her cheekbones. Her eyes that were gold, wide with wonder or half-closed when she was deliberating. Her slender neck, her elegant body. Her slim fingers, the wedding ring loose. She was always pushing it back, turning it, making sure it was there.

The wedding ring.

Steve felt a wave of dread engulf him. His mouth was dry. He could not swallow. It could not be. Surely not. It could not be over.

In a panic, he reached for the phone.

'Nigel.' His voice was harsh and raw. '*Boet*. I need to see you. Urgently.'

Nigel drove up to the house with a sense of foreboding.

It was in darkness. The outside light system that Steve was obsessive about, that he each night undertook to switch on and off himself, that he claimed was an essential security measure, was out. 'Keeps the bogey-men away,' he'd always joked with the girls.

Steve opened the front door. The hall was dark. Behind him was the ghostly outline of the curved staircase.

'Steve? What on earth's going on?' He saw the outline of his brother in the gloom.

'Come in.' Steve's voice sounded hollow.

'Switch on the lights. I can't see where I'm going.'

They went down the passage to the small lounge. The desk lamp cast a dull circle of light in the dark room. The drapes were drawn and bookshelves leaned oppressively from the shadows.

'Where's Laura?' he asked.

'She's not here.' Steve's elbows were on the desk, his face a dark shadow,

'Where is she?' Nigel watched his brother anxiously. This was not Steve. Not the confident brother he had relied on all the years he was growing up, the man he continued to hold in the highest regard. His clever, successful sibling. The admired wealthy businessman. The doting father.

The adored father of two lovely girls who'd praised him so publicly at their weddings. Who'd highlighted all his wonderful qualities, and told all what a fantastic dad he was, and what a happy home he and their mother had created, and spoken of their nurturing, love and concern in all the years that they were growing up. How these parents had created the perfect role model for marriage, the ideal example of a blissful union. A fine example for the girls to follow, to carry forward in their lives.

'She's gone. She left. I think she's left me.' Steve slumped forward onto the desk.

'What do you mean?' Nigel leaned towards him.

'She's not here.' Steve lifted his head. 'She's gone.'

The brothers' eyes became focused. Between them there had always only been the truth.

'I've been having an affair.'

'With who?'

'Carla. It's been going on for a few months.'

Nigel was astounded, disbelieving. Carla?

Steve read his mind. 'Yes. Carla. Crazy, hey?'

Nigel looked at him wordlessly.

Steve rushed on. 'It was the wrong thing to do. It was pure lust. She's a sexy woman and I was up for it. I'm not blaming her. I'm just as much at fault. I wanted it. We both wanted it. She set the scene and I went for it. I'm guilty. I know that.' He paused and swallowed hard.

Clearing his voice, he went on, 'I hoped to get away with it. That it would disappear as though it had never happened. The truth is, I'd had enough of Carla. I wanted my old life back, my life with Laura. I love Laura. You know that, Nige,' his eyes implored. 'I really do love her. So…' He paused.

'It was Laura's birthday. I booked at a restaurant for the two of us. I bought her flowers. I came home early. She was sitting here, where I'm sitting…' He indicated the chair he was in with a despairing hand. 'I came in here. She was just sitting and staring. I knew immediately that something was wrong. Nige, I'm in deep shit, man. I think this may be the end.'

'Carry on.' Nigel stared at his brother uncomprehendingly.

'She had a packet filled with photographs of the two of us…'

'What!' Nigel's long body pushed upright on the couch, his hands clasped between his knees.

'Ian had set it up. Hidden cameras. Photographs. He had the phone tapped. Recorded phone calls. He brought it here yesterday. Gave it all to Laura.'

'My God!'

'I know…'

'What did she do?'

'Well, as you can imagine, she was absolutely devastated. She wouldn't talk to me. I tried but she didn't want to know. She spent the night in Arielle's room. I was up the whole night. I must have dozed off this morning. When I went to look for her, the maid said she was gone.'

Steve desperately tried to see her, to talk to her. He phoned relentlessly. She would not take his calls. He'd knocked on the door of her mother's flat. She told him, 'No. She won't see you.' He'd caught a glimpse of her on the balcony. He called her name. She disappeared.

In desperation, he asked Nigel to see her. She held him in high regard, he said. 'Perhaps she'll listen to you.'

Her mother opened the door. Nigel saw her worried eyes sunken in deep furrows, her bagged grey cheeks, her thatch of chopped grey hair.

'Hello, Nigel.' Her voice was grave. 'Come in. Please. Laura's on the balcony.' He followed the sad back of the woman to a small balcony wreathed in petunias.

Laura stood up to greet him. She was less than slender, seemed taller, a long thin stem, her ashen skin taut across her wide cheek bones, her pale face a faded bloom. 'Hi.' Her eyes were expressionless. 'How are you?'

They sat facing each other. Below, a car revved. In the air was a waft of roasting meat. Along the uneven pavement, a line of gritty trees straggled.

'I'm OK. How are you?'

She did not bother to reply.

Her mother brought tea. Irritated, Laura noticed the ugly bone china teacups with matching teapot and milk jug. The stylised sprays of red roses. Not a single cup, saucer or side plate broken or chipped. Always locked away. Only used on special occasions. One of her mother's few treasures. A wedding gift displayed behind glass together with the crystal fruit bowl and the wine decanter.

Honestly, Ma, Laura thought, why have you hauled these out?

She poured the tea. Offered a buttery shortbread biscuit. Another of her mother's specialties. Her gaze was direct.

'Why have you come?'

He looked at her, his blue eyes frank and honest. Like Steve's, she thought. Then, with her heart lurching she realised, no. Not like Steve's… Not any more.

'Steve asked me to come. To talk to you.'

She was like a statue, her hands folded in her lap.

'Laura.' Nigel leaned forward, focusing on his words. 'He did wrong. Nobody knows that better than him. If he could go back in time and undo all this damage, he'd do it in a flash. But it happened. He bitterly regrets what he did. What they did.' He paused, his eyes intense, waiting for her reaction.

She did not respond.

'Laura. Please. Listen to me. What he did was bad. Very bad. But it was lust. Pure lust. Nothing more. She made herself available and he took advantage. Sure, they had a fling. But it's over. He doesn't want her. He wants you. He loves you. More than anything in the world he loves you. That's why I've come. Why I'm here. To ask you to forgive him. If you can. To give him another chance, Laura. He's devastated. Completely devastated. He says he can't be without you. He loves you. He wants you back.'

She was silent. Then reached for her bag. Took out the thick envelope. Handed it to him. 'Have a look at these…'

He only looked at the first two images. Stared at them. Wordlessly, he shook his head.

She watched his expression, her eyes yellow in the morning sun. Appalled, he met her gaze, saw her the lines of anguish around her tight mouth, her rigid shoulders, her white knuckles.

Her voice was harsh. 'You say he wants me back. Wants our life back. After that?' She glanced at the envelope on the table. 'Nigel, you're an intelligent person. You tell me! Can we can ever have our lives back again? After that? That was no fling! It was an intense love affair. As intimate as any marriage. During that time, he had no thought of me. No thought of our daughters, of our life together. Of all the years we shared. He only thought of himself, and of her…

'He cheated on me. Deceived me. And you say he loves me. After he destroyed what he promised to cherish? All our vows and promises. Gone. Totally destroyed. And you sit here and ask me to forgive him. To go back to him…'

She paused. Looked away. Became removed. As though she was trying to sought out her thoughts. Moments passed. The silence was heavy. Nigel waited.

She turned back to him, her eyes direct, her words deliberate. 'I can't do that.' She took a deep breath. 'My trust in Steve is gone. Smashed into millions of tiny pieces. No matter what he says, no matter how he feels, I'll never trust him again.'

Her voice sharpened. 'Marriage is based on trust. On trust, Nigel! That's number one. You can't have a marriage without trust. Can you?' She paused, gathering herself, trying to allay her emotions.

'No. Not only do I not trust him. I actually hate him. I hate him for what he's done to me. And not only to me. To Carolyn and Arielle. Our girls. Our daughters. He's shamed us. He's caused us pain and suffering. And terrible embarrassment. Everyone knows. My friends. Their friends. The whole community knows. They're all talking. It's caused a huge scandal. That's one thing – the scandal.

'But the girls are also hurting for us. We're their parents. The people they've always looked up to. They're devastated. Can't believe what's happened. And Arielle's expecting. This is terrible for her. I worry about her.' She paused.

There was a break in her voice. 'And my poor mother. She's beside herself. And my family. And yours?'

She waited. There were no words from him.

'They're all affected. Just think of the damage those two have caused. To so many people. People who loved them, who trusted them.'

She paused, trembling, then stood up and, to steady herself, placed her shaking hands flatly on the table. 'No, Nigel.' Her words were filled with purpose. 'I'm not interested in what he has to say. What he has done to me and the girls is inexcusable. Irredeemable. I will not go back to him. Not now. Not ever. It's over. Our marriage is over.'

She walked towards the balcony door. 'I've filed for divorce. The sooner the papers come through, the better.'

She ushered him ahead of her. She saw in Nigel the shape of Steve's head. Steve's resolute shoulders. Briefly she faltered. Then she said, with empathy, 'Thank you for coming. I know you meant well.' Her wan face hinted at a smile.

'That's OK. Laura, I'm so sorry. Really sorry. I would never have imagined that something like this could happen to the two of you. Knowing what you had.'

He reached out to take her hand. His eyes reached out to her. 'I understand how you feel. What this has done to you. But,' he tried again, 'I'll say it one more time. If you should find it within you to forgive him, to go back to him, to give him another chance, he'll be waiting for you. With open arms. So will we. We all want you back.'

She came into the apartment. Into light that poured in through tall blank windows and reflected on bare walls. The sun struck at blonde streaks in the floor, polished blocks of wood locked into a herringbone pattern. The ceilings were high and wide, the light fittings plain and square. The doors were solid imbuia. Brass door knobs gleamed.

None of this did she see.

She stood in the emptiness, her keys in her hand.

In silence and space surrounded by white walls.

Through the windows, plane trees, one on the lower lawn, the other up a few stone steps. Beds filled with shrubs and blooms, with perfumes and bees. A slatted bench, green paint peeling. A cracked cement bird bath.

At the kitchen window, a place for eating, for contemplating the distant mauve mountain range, the wide skies and a strip of ocean to the south. Over the road, the music school – an old house with many chimneys, comfortably sunk into lawns and shrubs, shaded by a gnarled and spreading oak and bordered by green playing fields.

A sense of space. Light and air.

From the bedroom, the green of the garden, shadows from a swaying palm tree.

From the time of Ian's fateful visit, Laura had been swamped by a range of intense emotions.

Anger, disbelief and an anguished sense of loss came to her at various times without warning. Claimed her sleep. Caused her to wake with a start in the dark hours, her face perspiring, her shoulders aching, her hands tightly clenched.

She hated Steve.

What he'd done was terrible. Horrific. Unforgivable. She'd needed to rid herself of him and anything to do with him.

To exorcise him from her life.

The divorce could not come quickly enough for her. There were exhausting meetings with her lawyer and accountant.

She had to decide what she would take from the house. What clothes? What books? What to do with her jewellery, all gifts from Steve. She did not want her rings and bracelets and necklaces. She wanted nothing associated with him. On the advice of her lawyer, she locked the items in a security box at the bank.

There were the phone calls. Calls from her daughters. From her mother. From her friends. Until she refused to answer the phone. Picked up the messages and answered only those that she chose to answer.

Even the calls from her daughters became a trial. The same questions, the pain in their voices, their overwhelming concern for her. She could not keep going over the same again and again.

She neglected to eat breakfast. She had a bite of a sandwich at lunchtime. In the evenings, she tried to swallow the soup her mother brought her.

Charged with nervous energy, she pushed through the days. Agitated, she paced, anxiously waiting for her next appointment.

By the time she moved into the flat, her clothes were hanging on her thin frame. Her face was pale, her eyes heavy. Her hair, always so lustrous and luxuriant, now hung dull and lifeless.

She sank onto the new grey leather couch in the lounge and stared at the blank walls without seeing them.

She sat without moving for a long time. Her mind numb. Her legs like lead.

Exhausted. Depleted. Drained.

Laura was as empty as the new space she'd created.

'Laura?' Her mother's elderly body bent over her with concern.

'What time is it?' Laura sat up, her eyes bleary, her hair hanging in greasy strands.

'Two o'clock,' Her mother glanced at her watch automatically.

'Two? Is it two? God. I've been sleeping all day…' Laura blinked, her gaze assaulted by the glare of white sunlight.

'Did you have a bad night?' Her mother watched her anxiously.

'Terrible. I tossed and turned for hours. Then I got up and made a cup of tea…' She turned to her mother, her voice as pale as her face. 'Tell me, Ma…' Words stumbled and tears began to run down her ashen face. 'What did I do wrong?'

'Laura, darling.' The old woman sat down beside her, her worn hand holding her daughter's thin hand, so thin that blue veins showed. 'You did nothing wrong.'

'I must've. I must've done something, or not done something, that drove him to it.' Her eyes were vacant. Her words rushed on. 'Maybe I never took enough care of myself. You know. Dressed up. Put on make-up. Had my hair done. Maybe he found me unattractive. He must've found me unattractive. That's why he got involved with her. She's very attractive. Glamorous. Sexy. And I'm plain.'

'No.' Her mother shook her head. 'You're not plain. You're beautiful. Much more beautiful than she is.'

'Well, he obviously didn't think so. And he likes to go out. To socialise. To move in those circles.' She turned her anguished gaze to her mother. 'I mean, I did it. I went along with it. But he knew it wasn't my scene. He could see that I didn't really enjoy all that.'

'You may not have liked it but you did it. You entertained. You had all those dinner parties. You went to all those shows. You dressed up and you looked gorgeous.'

Laura turned away. All the thoughts that tortured her during the night came back.

She told her mother, 'Maybe I was boring. Maybe he found me really boring. He never showed any interest in my work. Didn't want to know about my visits to the hospital. Said that it must be depressing to be with sick kids. He wasn't interested in hearing about in my writing. When people asked, he said, "She writes kids' stories." He was quite dismissive. Moved onto other conversations. He wasn't interested in the friends I made. Said they weren't really his type. "Too intellectual," he said, and he laughed when he said it.'

She started to cry. Convulsive sobs welled from her, overwhelming her. She leaned into the comfort of her mother's body and cried as though her heart was broken.

'I didn't want to lose him. You know that. I loved him more than I loved myself. I tried to do whatever I could to fit in.'

She looked away and said to herself, 'In the end it wasn't enough.'

She pushed dank strands of hair away from her tortured face. 'I wasn't enough. I just wasn't good enough.'

The mother cradled her child, imparting soothing words as they gently rocked together.

In the background, the murmurings, the mutterings.

'It looked OK, but, shows you, it wasn't a good marriage…'

His friends said, 'She didn't match up to him. Steve's a great guy. Hugely successful. Out there. She wasn't the right person for him.'

'She looks like a bit of a cold fish. Not much between the sheets.'

'Probably drove him to it.'

Her friends said, 'Laura was a loyal and devoted wife.'

'Steve was always eyeing the women. He may have had other flings. And even if he didn't, you could see that he had it in mind.'

'She did nothing wrong.'

'She's not to blame for his disgusting behaviour.'

'She's not the cause of his deception. That's who he is. A lying deceiving bastard.'

There were those who tried to be neutral: 'A midlife crisis.'

'These things happen.'

'They'll work through it.'

'In their own way.'

One way or another.

The page was blank. For some days, she stared at the void, at an empty sky. It did not matter to her that nothing came to mind, that there were no words. For the time being, the space was infused with peace.

She pushed back in her chair and walked to the lounge. Vivid leaves faced her in swaths of whispering green.

From her bedroom window, palm leaves swayed.

Air flowed.

There was birdsong, bees and the high pitch of cricketsong. Or silence.

The blank page waited.

She did not encourage visitors.

Except, perhaps, for her mother. Unobtrusively, the elderly woman sat on the balcony, sipping tea, her knitting bag beside her, her needles clicking. Her well worn hands, knobbled, freckled, creased. Sometimes it was embroidery. Or a magazine. Her passive face sunk into friendly folds, waiting to smile. Her green eyes were mild.

There was her comfortableness, her soothing calmness.

Her sweetness, her kindness.

Her gentle disposition.

What she really wanted was to be alone.

To watch the night deepen, the moon riding, the stars becoming sharp.

To see the dawn pushing against the horizon in pale shades of grey. To watch the miracle of sunrise, the blaze of fiery red and crimson and cerise, ruddy and blushing and rosily glowing as the gold disc of sun peeped over the range then rose splendidly in the flaming sky.

To sleep when sleep called.

To curl into the couch in the middle of the morning when light was striking the eastern windows, to open her eyes to sunbeams breaking in from the west.

To eat her first meal of the day when it should have been her last.

To let cool water flow down her face and through her hair and over her body. To remain in her dressing gown.

For it to be summer or winter. Oranges or grapes.

She was not in a hurry. Time could take its time.

The weather sharpened.

Wind lashed around corners and moaned through narrow lanes. Trees shivered and shed their leaves.

The sky was ice-blue.

Laura wandered around the shop. She saw barley. There were black-eyed beans.

She chopped an onion, carrots and celery. It felt strange to be slicing vegetables. How long was it since she last cooked?

How ridiculous that she'd allowed that woman to take over her kitchen. How did that happen? Steve said that he was going to elevate her. That she was now the privileged wife of a rich man. She needed to behave like one.

'We'll get ourselves a cordon bleu cook,' he told her. 'She'll chop the onions…' He never liked the onion smell on her hands.

'How good it feels to slice an onion,' she said to herself. No one will ever stop me from doing that again.'

She soaked ripe red tomatoes in boiling water. They burst in their skins. She peeled and chopped them and tipped them into the pot. Then sweet chunks of butternut. A handful of parsley, some chives and rosemary all growing in abundance in the garden, a small red chili, some rich stock, the soaked barley, the black beans.

Rich aromas from the bubbling pot filtered through the flat.

A comforting bowl of thick warm soup. A slice of rye bread spread with butter.

That terrible evening continued to haunt her. She remembered stumbling blindly down the passage towards the front door, pulling it open and being assaulted by blinding sheets of black rain, stumbling up the stairs and holding the walls.

She'd found herself in Arielle's room, completely numb and uncomprehending.

Did she really see those images? They came to her blurred yet burningly clear. Steve and Carla together in that thick envelope.

And the recordings. Ian had said they were telephone conversations. What did they say?

She remembered trembling uncontrollably. She'd seen Steve's outline, heard his voice but not what he was saying, turning away from the glass of water he'd brought for her.

She'd not been able to recall how the envelope came to be in her bag…

That evening haunted him.

Steve had stared at the photographs. Urgently he picked up the thick wad and, one by one, carefully studied them. There was no mistaking what they represented. Half-dressed or naked, in intense intimacy, their bodies intertwined, their mouths, their hands, the desire in their eyes. It was all there.

He'd dropped them onto the desk then dropped his head in his hands. There was nothing to be said. Nothing that would diminish this evidence.

There were also the recordings. Those terrible telephone conversations. Steve had stared blankly ahead.

There was no way out of this. Nothing that could mitigate the devastation that faced him. No answer to Laura's anguished cry, '*Steve. What have you done?*'

He wandered around his mausoleum, along the endless passages lined with ivory walls decorated with framed canvases – art and artists, his mother claimed, that they could not afford to be without.

'Wonderful,' she told her son. And, as an aside, 'Such a good investment.'

Blankly staring with red-rimmed eyes, with lips set in a grim thin line and blue shadow covering his jaw, his tall gaunt figure walked into empty bedrooms that bore evidence of his daughters. A pair of high-heeled shoes half hidden under a bed, pearl earrings in a small porcelain dish, an array of half used bottles of perfume, jars of face cream.

He stood motionless, his arms hanging. They were gone. His girls. Married and living in another country.

Their chatter and laughter and running footsteps had become lost echoes.

All that wondrous commotion was gone.

But he'd had Laura.

And yes. He'd also had Carla.

For a time, he believed that he could have both of them.

Now they were gone – Carla by his design, and Laura because of Carla.

Unsure of himself, he held onto the banister.

The Blue Room, lustreless, was enveloped in weak white light that seeped through the tulle drapes. He glanced around, not registering, until he came to the carved head of the crevassed old man whose age-old eyes met his gaze, whose pleated lips accused, seeming to ask, 'What did you do?'

Dust settled undisturbed on surfaces.

The maids, aware that no one was watching, had become lazy.

Relishing in their idleness, they sat at the kitchen table eating thick slices of bread and butter lashed with apricot jam, and noisily sucked at mugs of sweet tea. The oats bubbled, and the nauseating smell of boiled meat and onions wafted unchecked through the house.

The gardener, who was told, 'Looks like the madam is gone,' noted that his master no longer inspected the hedges and shrubs. He bought a bottle of cheap wine and settled down under a bush behind the pool fence. The pool, always pristine, now had leaves floating, becoming rotten, and sinking to the bottom in slimy brown smudges.

From the small sitting room came the persistent ringing of the phone. Steve ignored it. It rang again. He sat down at the desk, looked at the receiver, then stared at Laura's pens grouped together in a clay container.

He felt the shape of his wife in the chair, and, with his cupped hand, held its carved wooden arm as she used to do.

'Steve?' It was Carla.

'Oh. Hi.'

'How are you?' Her voice was hesitant.

'Terrible,' he answered tersely. He was silent, then asked, 'And you?'

'Shocking. Absolutely awful.'

Steve did not respond.

She asked, 'How's Laura?'

'Laura? She's moved out.' His voice was hollow. 'And Ian?'

'He here. But he's moved out of the bedroom. He's sleeping in one of the kids' rooms.'

He heard a break in her voice.

'He's going to divorce me. Calls me a slut and a whore. Says he hates the sight of me.' Then added, 'He hates you too. Says you're a real bastard.'

Steve nodded, acknowledging Ian's damning opinion of them. He said, 'So what will you do?'

'I don't know.' Her voice faltered. 'I really don't. 'He says he's going to screw me into the ground. Give me the barest minimum. Promised me that I will definitely not be living the life of a rich divorcee.' Her voice faded. 'But he'll have to provide for us. That's the law. He's told the kids. All about us. I begged him not to.' She sounded as though she was crying. 'They're absolutely distraught. They can't believe what's going on. Of course they blame me. And of course, they're right. I'm going to lose them. They'll all end up hating me.'

The magnitude of their deed and its appalling ramifications loomed massively before them.

Steve's head rested wearily in his hand. 'Jesus. What a fuck-up,' he groaned. 'What the hell have we done?'

'We made love.' Carla whispered. 'That's what we did. We wanted each other.'

He did not answer.

'Are you sorry? Sorry that we did what we did?' Carla's voice was barely audible. 'I mean… For me, it was amazing being with you. Steve? Are you sorry?'

'Am I sorry? Of course I'm sorry. I regret it. Every moment of it. If I could have that time back, I'd run a mile. What we did destroyed us. Destroyed our families. My life's ruined. I've wrecked my marriage. I've brought shame on Laura and my girls. For what, Carla? For a bit of hot sex? Yes, it was good. I'm not denying that. But I had good sex with my wife. She's an amazing woman. A beautiful woman. I didn't need to stray. I had everything I needed from Laura. I didn't need to mess around. Not with you or with anyone else.'

Carla cried. 'I thought you felt something for me. Something more than just sex. It meant so much to me. Everything to me. More than my marriage. Maybe even more than my children. I never slept with you for sex. I love you, Steve. You know that I love you. I love you more than anything in the world. I always have, and I always will.'

Steve paused. Then said, slowly and clearly, 'I hear what you say, and I'm really sorry that you rate your feelings for me above your husband and your kids. But I've never led you to believe that I love you. Not once have I ever said that I love you.'

'Perhaps you can learn to love me,' she pleaded. 'Perhaps when this is all over, when the dust settles, we can be together.'

'Carla, you're not listening. I've told you. And I'll tell you again, I love Laura. She's the only woman I love. The only woman I've ever loved. Laura. My wife. I will love her until the day I die.'

Nigel recommended a psychologist, a fresh-faced man with a pink skin and gleaming eyes. There was a jauntiness about his rotund figure. A joyful energy. It seemed to Steve that he was about to leap out of his chair, burst into song, skip about his office.

'Is he for real?' he asked his brother after their introduction.

'He's for real,' Nigel confirmed. 'Behind that *joie de vivre* is a very sharp guy. He sees everything. He hears everything. Go along with him. Talk to him. He'll clarify things for you.'

'Start from the beginning,' said the therapist. 'Tell me what happened.'

Steve told him of the relationship they had when they were young and single. How, despite everyone's expectations that he would become engaged to Carla, he'd chosen Laura. How devastating that was for Carla at that time.

He described the evening, all those years later, when he'd sat across the table from her at a dinner party. The stirrings between them.

How he thought about her on the way home. Her eyes that had flirted, her slow smile, the way she held her fork in her small hand, her crimson-tipped nails.

He remembered that Laura had asked if he was OK. 'You seem distracted,' she'd commented as they'd driven through the shadowy streets.

He told the therapist how Ian had contacted him, somewhat apologetically, saying that he knew that they did not do 'small jobs', but that Carla had insisted that he at least enquire. They wanted to build a conservatory.

Steve had immediately accepted the job that was out of line with their work. 'We do buildings,' he explained. Multistorey buildings. Not additions. Not conservatories.'

'So you were wired in. You were both already emotionally involved. Do you see that? You wanted to reconnect. You both contrived in your own ways to make that connection happen.'

Steve described how he had gone to the house to check the work, something his foreman was well qualified to do. He did this impulsively and compulsively. She was constantly in his thoughts. He needed to see her again.

He described Carla to the therapist. How she looked. What she wore. The way she walked. Her voice. Her perfume. The day he found her lying at the pool.

'You realise that she'd never given up on you. Her sense of desertion when you severed your relationship all those years ago must have had a profound effect on her. There were probably times that she was filled with intense longing for you. May have even made long term plans to recapture what she'd lost. When she saw you again, all that passion she had for you resurged.'

They explored why Steve, an experienced and worldly man, had been so willing.

'You probably had an emotional disconnect at that time with your wife. It's not to say that you didn't love her. Your love for her was present, but it wasn't burning brightly enough.'

'I was taking her for granted,' Steve agreed. 'But I loved her. I've always loved her.'

'Love is a living thing,' said the therapist. 'It needs constant nourishment.'

Steve wanted to know what had happened that did not allow him to simply walk away.

The therapist told him, 'Your nature is such that you set your goals and you achieve what you want. In many ways, this has served you well. I understand that you're a very successful man. Highly regarded in the business world. For you, this affair was yet another challenge. Another goal.'

The therapist said that illicit affairs are sneaky, deceptive, immoral and unethical. 'You must have known what you were doing was wrong, But you were prepared to take a gamble, because you've always done exactly what you want. Always had your own way, so to speak. And, because you usually come out on top, you did not for one moment anticipate losing this gamble.'

He told Steve that the rush from the prospect of a new lover brings out selfishness. 'That's why you had no thought for your family, or for any possible adverse consequences for your actions. You tasted forbidden fruit. You were thrilled by it. In this heightened state of excitement, this euphoria, you both lost touch with reality. You wanted each other and you sought every opportunity to be together.'

He said that besides unfettered impulses, affairs also lead unrealistic expectations. 'That is why, for example, Carla expected you to leave Laura for her.'

'Will Laura come back to me?' he implored.

The therapist said that sexual infidelity is very damaging to the aggrieved partner and to a relationship. 'But for women,' he went on, 'the emotional infidelity they perceive to have taken place is even more distressing than the physical involvement. Conversely, for men the sexual infidelity is most distressing. Laura will go through much anguish,' he said. She will feel deep hurt. She will go through depression, anxiety and distress. She may see herself as unattractive and undesirable. She may feel insecure and lacking confidence.'

He looked at Steve out of mild, kind eyes. 'Considering what she has gone through, I would expect her feeling for you to be hostile, perhaps vengeful. She will perceive that you have brought shame upon her and your children. She may be nauseated by you. Find you repulsive. Right now your relationship is in a state of dissolution.'

Steve had not considered that Laura might think of him in these ways – being nauseated by him, or finding him repulsive.

The therapist told him, 'You've achieved a great deal in your life. You reached an age and a stage where you looked around and wondered what was left for you to do? You may have seen your life as dull. Your sex life may have become routine. Communication between you and Laura was insignificant. Your wife may have noticed, but being, as you have described, an acquiescent person, she may not have wanted to stir things up. And so she became even more reticent and absorbed herself with her writing.'

Desperately he asked whether, given time, she would change her mind? Come back to him? Come back to the marriage?

'Can your relationship be resurrected? It depends on whether she's able to forgive you. And, if so, to what extent.'

He asked himself, why, at that fateful dinner, he was not paying attention to his wife. Laura who had looked so lovely. Who'd smiled at him? Who'd looked deeply into his eyes, searching for his love.

What had happened for him to reject his wife for a woman he'd rejected all those years before?

He knew that he'd felt Carla's presence in a disturbing way. She was using her eyes, her smile, the turn of her head, her shoulders in a way that was familiar to him. They were her signals. She was using them on him again.

He'd become excited. Why?

Because he was restless. He'd found Laura wanting.

He wanted glamour. Women who glittered and glowed. Who showed the clefts between their breasts. He would find himself watching such women in restaurants and enjoying their glances. He recalled a woman who sat next to him at the theatre. Her skirt was split, revealing her thighs. He was enthralled and he knew that she, a perfect stranger, was aware of the effect she was having on him.

He watched women everywhere, whether Laura was with him or not. It bothered her. She found his distractions disconcerting, but in his mind it was harmless.

'I'm only looking,' he told her.

He now realised that his interest in other women and the arousal they created in him made him mentally and emotionally unfaithful to his wife long before his affair.

Laura, who sat at her desk in a loose sweater with her hair in a ponytail and her pale scrubbed face, had faded from his focus.

Their love was there but not burning brightly enough.

She would not see him. She wanted to divorce him.

He'd formulated a plan. A way forward. Rehearsed it in his mind. Over and over.

He needed to implore her to forgive him. To swear to God that he'd become the kind of husband she deserved. Never upset her again. Not in any way. To assure her that they'd find their way back to the great love they'd shared, the love he knew existed between them. Because she was a wonderful woman. The only woman he'd ever loved. She was the love of his life.

He would ask her to let him prove these sentiments. To give them another chance. Not to throw away what was irreplaceable.

Please, Laura, he'd beg, let's put this behind us. I know that I strayed. That I'm guilty of a terrible betrayal. I deeply regret it. I'm asking you to please give me a chance to again become the man you married. I'll answer any questions you may ask of me truthfully. I will not hide anything from you. I'll tell you whatever you want to know, no matter how painful it will be.

I will then be at your side so that we may go through the pain together. And the grief. I will be there for as long as it takes. We'll embark on a path of healing.

I promise you that we'll come through this terrible time stronger than before. Because what we have is so strong that nothing can destroy it. We will do it together. We will beat it.

All I need is for you to give me another chance.

Because I love you.

Laura.

Please...

I love you... I love you...

The therapist's words echoed in his mind. 'You were a perfect candidate for an affair. Even if Laura had suspected you, confronted you and demanded to know what was going on, in your crisis state you would not have been listening. Also, your daughters are now married and have left home. You both needed to adjust to the "empty nest". That, too, may cause emotional stress that, in turn, can lead to existential thinking.

'You're in the middle of your life. You had a great yearning to live your life to its fullest. You wanted to rejuvenate your sex life. Feel young again. You're a man used to taking risks. Having an affair is one of the riskiest things a man can do. Your affair was stimulating and exciting. You burned with desire. You let your emotions take hold of you.'

Nauseated by him. Repulsed by him. No.

Please God.

No.

He cried.

He who had never cried sobbed uncontrollably.

News of the two impending divorces was rampant.

There were those who claimed that they'd sensed something at the dinner party.

Someone who'd seen Steve's car outside Carla's house.

'Poor Laura,' they clucked sympathetically. 'Such a lovely person. Didn't deserve this. That Carla's such a bitch.'

'She took her revenge,' said others.

'Laura took Steve from her. Now she's taken Steve from Laura.'

'An eye for an eye and a tooth for a tooth,' came from someone who chose to quote the Bible.

Summer faded. Evenings lengthened and chilled. In the garden, brittle leaves danced over dead heads of blooms, and the songs of insects dwindled.

For Laura, the change was welcome. She'd found the summer trying. The air had been heavy and oppressive, the light too bright, the days too long. The rooms, blasted with shafts of sun, became uncomfortably warm. She'd sat on the garden bench one afternoon but the shade of the plane tree gave no relief. Clusters of bougainvillea – orange, cerise, crimson – burgeoning luxuriantly against the red-brick walls, flamed like a raging fire. Even the grass acquired a brittle green glassiness that hurt her eyes.

In the evening air, she sat on her balcony, a woollen shawl wrapped around her shoulders. The dusk blurred the garden into grey and brown shadows. Below, the rustle of leaves. Ahead, the swaying palm.

She watched the outlines of chimney pots on the crenellated roof of the building next door, a building that resembled a castle with turrets and arched gateways and doors fitted with big brass trimmings.

The sky darkened, stars stationed, and there was the slow majestic journey of the moon.

She watched the lighted windows surrounding the garden. Sometimes a face in a window. Or the shadow of someone moving across a room.

From the flat above her were the indistinguishable words of the evening news. From another, the faint sound of music.

The scent of rosemary gently floating as though through glass.

She sat, still and silent, in the long hushed night, until the first grey fingers of dawn emerged.

It did not matter.

She had the time.

She took the time.

The days.

The nights.

The weeks.

The months.

And all the time she was gently healing…

When the words came, they were unstoppable.

She lay in bed and stared at the black sky brilliantly perforated with stars and a crescent moon. She tried to distinguish the outline of the whole moon. It was there. An almost invisible circle.

Her mind was alert. Thoughts flashed brightly. Words formed.

She could see, hear and then speak the first sentence of the first page. She wrote it down quickly, urgently.

She closed her eyes but sleep evaded her.

Exhilarated, she pushed her hair from her face and, barefooted, padded to her desk. The sentence led to a paragraph, and then a page.

Thoughts surged. Words shaped around them. Feelings, emotions, experiences, all that was bottled up within her, flowed.

The pages filled effortlessly.

When she crept back under the duvet with aching eyes and numbed feet, the moon had disappeared.

Her mother noticed. She's looking better. Brighter. More herself. She's got a bit of colour. Not so drawn. She's eating better.

Reluctant to comment in case she upset Laura, her mother waited and silently observed.

Her daughter, her wonderful girl, had gone through such a terrible time. She'd wondered whether she'd ever be herself again.

Night after night, the woman had sat with endless cups of tea dwelling on the awful turn of events in Laura's life. Wondering how it would all end.

Seeing how ill she'd become. How thin. How pale.

Many times, she clasped her hands together and turned her anguished face to the ceiling as though it was heaven and pleaded, 'Look after her, God. Please, please look after her. Help her. She needs you. I can't do this on my own.'

And now, look at her. Better. Much better.

Again she glanced heavenwards and clasped her hands together. 'Thank you, God. Thank you.'

'I'm writing again,' Laura told her.

The mother smiled, wanting to ask, 'What? What are you writing?' Instead she said, 'Oh. That's nice, darling.'

'Yes, it is nice. I'm enjoying it.'

'That's good. I'm so pleased.'

'I'm finding it easy. The thoughts and words just flow. I've done quite a bit.'

'Wonderful. I'm so pleased. You're a good writer, Laura,' she added timidly.

'I don't know if I'm good. But I feel good doing it. It's cathartic, the writing. It's like I'm letting out everything that's inside me.'

'That's good.' Her mother nodded, thoughtfully choosing her words and the tone of her voice.

Laura, so fragile, so delicate, had closed the door on everyone. Even her daughters… She did not want to speak to them. Her conversations with them were one-sided, their chatter, their news, their questions from across the ocean.

Laura said 'Yes' or 'No'. Sometimes no answer. Silence.

And so her mother became even more cautious. She did not want to be shut out of her daughter's life.

In fact, Laura needed her. She was the only person she needed.

She'd sometimes leave her bed, walk holding onto walls to the dining room, and watch the rounded shape of her mother's shoulders and her grey head through the balcony window. Clutching the back of a chair, she'd listen to the reassuring click of the knitting needles.

Words Sentences Paragraphs Pages
    Thoughts Feelings Emotions
    Impressions Memories
    Characters Personalities
    Pain

A jumble of words. Jumbled thoughts.
    She knew there was a lot that needed to be fixed.
    She'd do it.
    She'd work through it.
    She'd get it right.

It said what she'd wanted to say.
    It was all there.
    Her soul was there.

She recalled her teacher's words all those years ago.

'When you've experienced life, you'll be able to write. You've got the tools. You now need the years. The highs. The lows. Life is the lesson for any serious writer. Your life will teach you what you need to know.'

The Italia overflowed with patrons. Luigi, capacious in his apron, had accommodated the crowd by bringing in extra chairs. People had to squeeze past to reach their tables.

'Can't complain about business!' Someone patted him on his well-padded shoulder.

'Who's complainin'?' grinned the rotund owner. 'Come. Sit. Eat.'

It was Carla's birthday. She'd invited her sons to join her and their sister for brunch. The boys lived with Ian and, although they still bore her some resentment, agreed to come. She'd also asked Steve. His initial response had been unenthusiastic but then he thought why not and decided he would go.

Since his divorce, he preferred to be alone. He'd sold the huge house, had disposed of the furniture and the art, and had moved into an apartment. He filled his days with work, going to the gym, and riding his bicycle through the suburbs until he was exhausted and ready to drop into bed.

He'd tried every avenue to reconcile with Laura, but she was determined to divorce him. The months that followed were bleak. He faced judgement from every side, except from his brother, and his mother, who had always thought that she was not the right girl for him. 'I said so from the word go,' she told all who would listen.

But the greatest judgement he served on himself. He did not attempt to excuse himself. He was to blame. He'd had the affair because that's what he'd wanted. He always got what he wanted. That's who he'd been.

And now. Look at him. On his own. Without Laura. Yes, he told himself, that's what you did. You destroyed your life.

There were times that he was angry with Carla. But he could not blame her for trying. She was in love with him and had never given up on them being together.

He'd visited her in the cottage that she shared with her daughter. Again he had to tell her that although they were both on their own, he would never marry her. He loved Laura. Only Laura. He told her how he had his wife – no, his ex-wife – in mind every day. She was the first thought he woke up to and his last thought as he fell asleep.

He said that he and Carla could be friends, but nothing more.

He joined her and her children at the Italia at their table in the back corner of the restaurant.

The doorway framed the silhouette of a woman, her hair a rich chestnut in the light. She was slim in black leather pants and a soft cream blouse. In one hand, she carried a briefcase. With her free hand, she waved to a table near the window. She walked through the crowd, her face flushed from the unusually warm weather. Two men at a table rose to their feet to greet her. Pushing her lustrous hair away from her face, she smiled as they kissed her on both cheeks. She bent to kiss the woman who was seated.

Steve's heart lurched. It was Laura. He saw her smile and he thought that he could hear her laugh. He could see her profile, her lips, the light slanting from her cheekbones, her hair, thick and lustrous, framing her face, falling to her shoulders.

Laura.

Again, instinctively, Carla followed his gaze. 'Go and say hello to her,' she said softly.

He stumbled to his feet. 'Yes. I think I will.' He excused himself and found his way to her table from the far end of the restaurant.

'Laura?' he said hesitantly.

She glanced up, her lovely face smiling. 'Steve,' she replied with some warmth. 'How're you?'

A flood of tenderness for her flowed though him. 'I'm OK. And you?' He smiled down at her.

'I'm fine. Meet my friends. Tony Hanson, and Pierre and Suzette Lamond. My ex, Steve…'

How confident she seems, how self-assured, Steve thought.

'Tony makes movies…' she smiled.

'What did you say your name was?' Steve asked.

'I didn't. Laura did. But the name's Hanson, Tony Hanson.'

'Tony Hanson.' Steve looked at him. 'The film director?'

'That's me,' the man smiled. 'That's what I do.'

'You're well known.' Steve watched him intently. 'I mean, you're famous.'

'Tony wants to make a movie of my book.' Laura intervened.

'Oh. Really. Fantastic.' Steve focused on the director, feeling a rush of protection for Laura as though they were still married. 'And how far down the line is that?'

'Way down the line,' the director responded. 'In fact, the deal is done.'

'You mean you've signed the contracts?' Steve's business senses were now alert. Concerned, he turned to Laura. 'Who's looking after your interests?'

Laura answered him coolly. 'My lawyer. My accountant. They're managing my affairs.'

'Well, I hope you're being properly looked after.'

'I am.' She turned away.

'She is,' echoed the man called Tony. 'I can assure you. Very well looked after.'

Laura exchanged glances with those at the table then looked up. 'You'll have to excuse us, Steve.' She was now dismissive. 'We have some matters to discuss.'

'Oh. Right. Sure. Didn't mean to interrupt.'

She did not answer.

The flat was quiet in the autumn dusk.

Laura was soothed by a gentle light that filtered from the garden, and the sweep of brown sky stretching to the distant mountains. She heard birds calling to each other, one distinct repetitive sound answered by another repetitive sound. Messages being sent by birds around the garden and across the skies. She watched a bird perched on a telephone pole. Its head bobbed and it hopped to face her, then hopped to face away from her. It was joined by others. For a short while they crowded, chirping to each other, then flew off in tandem, becoming a pattern of black dots.

She ran the bath water, tipping a generous amount of sweet smelling oil into the bath. Standing in the rising steam, she soaped herself generously then sank back into the soothing warmth, her eyes closed in the lulling lap of water.

She thought about Steve. How he'd come across to speak to her.

How Suzette had reached across and touched her hand with delicate fingers and said in her beguiling way, 'He still loves you.'

How she had answered, 'Yes. I know.'

'He seems a sensitive man,' Suzette suggested.

'Sensitive? No. Not really. I've never known him to be sensitive.'

'Maybe not before. But men change as they become older. And women…'

Laura recalled Pierre interjecting. 'My wife studied Jung. She told me. Anima. It's when a man becomes older, he expresses himself through his feminine inner personality. And the opposite happens for women – animus. They use their masculine inner feelings.' He turned with a tender expression to face his wife. 'Am I right, *cherie*? Did I say that right?'

'Yes, Pierre. That is what Jung said. So, perhaps he is more gentle now, more sensitive, your ex-husband,' she said softly. 'And you are,' she paused, 'how you say – more hard, more tough.'

'More in charge,' Laura corrected her. 'Steve's a dominating man. Always wanted his own way. I used to try to please him. To do what he wanted. Now I'm in charge of myself, I've become my own person.'

'You are happy, my Laura?' Suzette's beautiful eyes were quizzical. 'You are more happy on your own?'

'I'm content. And I'm fulfilled. And I have peace in my life. If that is being happy, then, yes, I suppose I'm happy.'

She slipped into the silken comfort of a Chinese wrap, tying the sash around her slim waist, and, bare-footed, padded to the kitchen to make a sandwich and tea. From the window, the stars were out, bright in the nearly winter skies, the riding moon oval, reflected in its own blue shadow.

She watched a cat skulking blackly along the wall.

The lights of a car, just parked, were turned off. In the dark driveway, a man stepped out. For a moment, he seemed familiar.

The doorbell rang.

'Who is it?' she called.

'Steve. It's Steve.'

They sat at the table in the window in the glow from a small table lamp. Street lights cast funnels of light onto the pavement and reflected through the glass pane. There was a white beam from the moon.

She faced him, her face luminous, her eyes clear and golden, her lips pale. Shadows slanted from her wide cheekbones. Her wrap parted revealing her shapely legs. There were her bare feet. There was the cleft between her soft full breasts.

He saw all of her. He felt her quiet presence. He listened to her gentle voice. Never had he known her to be more beautiful.

She told him that her book had been successful. It was translated into twelve languages. He said that he knew, that he'd followed its progress with great interest. That he was delighted for her. Very proud of her. He said that he'd always thought that she had it in her.

She answered that it was a pity he'd never told her that before.

Of course, he answered. He should have. He'd made many mistakes. He knew that. He should have said more, shown more. He could see that now. He deeply regretted it. If he could go back in time, he would have done things differently, better, given her more of what she needed, what she deserved.

But he'd always loved her. She knew that, didn't she? He still loved her. He would always love her.

She sat in silence in the shadows. She saw his anguished face, his hair that was silver in the night light, his hands that were clasped. She saw the slump of his broad shoulders. She heard his despair.

She told him in her quiet voice that she was leaving. Was emigrating. She was going to join the girls.

'What!' He was flabbergasted. 'When?'

She stood with him in the lighted doorway. 'Will I see you before you go?'

She did not answer him. Instead, she took his face into her hands and looked deeply into his eyes. For a few moments, she was silent.

'When I met you,' she said softly, 'I would look into your eyes and tell myself that I could see your soul. It seemed to me to be a beautiful soul, pure and good.'

She searched his eyes. 'I can't see it now.'

She paused, then stepped away from him, her eyes filled with sadness. 'No, Steve,' she said gently, 'I won't see you before I leave. There's no point.'

The plane rose in a flawless sky. Below was Table Mountain, its protective flanks surrounding the suburbs of Cape Town.

Her eyes travelled over the city, its harbour and beaches. The place that had been her home.

She was leaving nothing behind.

She felt light and free. Free to be. In a new place. With her daughters. With their families.

Smiling, Laura accepted an apple juice from a smiling air hostess, sipped the sweet drink and closed her eyes.

There was only the soft drone of the plane's engines and the comforting rustle of someone's newspaper.

They were there to meet her, Carolyn and Arielle, with excited eyes , pushing in front of the waiting crowd. They rushed forward, threw their arms around her, planted kisses on her cheeks, took her hand luggage and held her hands, one on either side of her.

She cried. 'Oh, my darlings. I'm so happy to see you. So happy.'

Arielle gently wiped away her tears. 'Don't cry, Ma,' she said softly.

She bought an apartment on the first floor of a house that had been converted into two units.

It faced the ocean, an expanse of changing blues that stretched into the far distance to meet a blue horizon. Light and sea breezes flowed through the windows.

A cosy room off the lounge instantly became her workplace. She felt secure in the tight space where, after placing her desk and book-shelves, there was just enough room to swivel her chair.

From that window was a view of the street, quiet and wide with green pavements and lush trees, and a row of handsome houses.

People passed – a man with his dog, a mother pushing a pram, an elderly couple arm in arm.

Sometimes she heard a car. Sometimes a plane.

Each morning before sunrise, she walked along the cliff, watching the sun reach into crimson skies and the jewelled sea dance in sparkles of ruby and tourmaline.

Some days clouds, swollen and ominous, hung in a dark sky. Rumbles and deafening crashes of thunder followed jagged lightning – vicious daggers that struck and pierced the sullen ocean.

She was in awe of electric storms, fearful of their ferocity, and en-thralled by their might.

She resolved to get a dog. Her daughters suggested a poodle.

'They don't shed hair,' Carolyn told her. 'Their fur is wool.'

They knew of a breeder. They would take her. A puppy the colour of champagne, or perhaps a grey one.

'They're adorable, especially after they've had their first poodle cut.'

She thanked them and said she would let them know.

On a Sunday morning, she drove to the pound. There were many dogs in cages. She thought she might find one that looked like Trixie. She came upon a funny-looking little dog with a sweet face and innocent eyes that seemed to look right through her.

'I think I like that dog,' she told the attendant. 'Is it a he or a she?'

'A female,' he answered. 'Spayed and microchipped. All ready to go.'

'How old is she?'

The dog watched her intently.

'Very young. Maybe a year old. We can't give an exact age.'

'Do you know anything about her? Her previous owner perhaps?'

'No, we don't. But we think she was treated well. There's nothing in her nature to suggest otherwise.'

'Does she have a name?'

'We call her Bon Bon. We think it suits her. She's a very sweet little animal.'

For a long moment, they watched each other – Laura and Bon Bon. The dog's ears went into sharp points and her tail moved hesitantly from side to side. Laura reached through the cage to pat her. Bon Bon jumped up in a frenzy of excitement.

Laura laughed. 'She really is very sweet.'

For a few minutes, she quietly observed the dog. Then nodded, 'I'll take her.'

She swam in the sea. She swam in the saltwater sea pool. She held onto the railings and let the waves wash over her.

She sat on the beach and turned her face to the warm comfort of the sun. She listened to the lapping waves.

She watched the seagulls devouring a discarded packet of potato chips. She sipped hot sweet tea.

She thought about the latest chapter of her new novel. Made notes in her head. Thought about words, about phrases… Became excited about the direction the story would take…

Peace came to her.

Joy.

Happiness.
Contentment.
Fulfilment.

Carolyn and Arielle had been concerned about their mother's impending emigration, that she was middle-aged, divorced, on her own… They saw her as someone who had always been protected.

They'd not been with her during the long months of suffering she'd endured following her break-up with Steve. They'd learned of her rehabilitation from a distance.

They heard and read of her subsequent literary success from afar.

They had not witnessed first-hand the transformation that had taken place in her. They thought that she might be vulnerable. That she would find a new life in a new country difficult.

'We'll have to be around, you know, to keep an eye…' they'd told each other.

They sat on her patio eating salad rich with tuna, eggs, olives and feta cheese. Told her how incredible they thought she was. How proud they were of how she'd coped.

'You're fantastic, Ma. You've settled so well. Taken to everything like a duck to water…'

'We're thrilled with you. So pleased to see you happy…'

'Thanks, darlings. I am happy. I feel very fortunate. I have everything I could possibly want. Most important – I have all of you. I'm a very lucky woman.'

'We're lucky too, to have you.'

'Ma?' Arielle hesitated. 'Can I ask you something?'

'Yes. Of course. What do you want to ask me?'

'I want to ask you whether you ever think about Dad?'

Laura put down her fork and looked away.

Steve.

She did not answer.

Arielle rushed on. 'He always asks after you. Whenever we speak.

Always wants to know how you are. Tells us all the time to keep an eye on you. To see that you're OK.'

'Does he? And what do you say?'

'We tell him as it is. That you're fine. Really doing well. That you have a lovely apartment. That you have a little dog.'

'That you're busy with your writing. That you go on long walks. That you swim.'

'And what does he say?'

'He's pleased. Really pleased. He says he wants everything to go well for you and for you to be happy. I think he misses you.'

'Do you ever think about him, Ma?'

'No. I've put him out of my mind. He's not the person that I knew. Not the man I fell in love with, that I married. So, no, I don't think about him. He's not a part of my life any more.'

'Will you see him when he comes at the end of the year?'

'Of course I'll see him.' She smiled. Her eyes smiled. She reached out to touch their hands. 'I'll see him at you... And at you...'

Steve drove past the apartment staring at the drawn blinds on the windows. He turned the car round and drove back again.

Laura had never drawn the blinds. Once, he'd driven by on impulse and had caught the passing shadow of her. At other times, a light from the windows.

Now there were drawn blinds.

He experienced an acute sense of loss.

Painfully, he realised how much he'd relied on occasionally seeing her, and how much he missed hearing her voice when they'd exchanged messages from their children. How he'd clung to those few inter-actions, however trite. Now – nothing.

He was introduced to other women, some of them pretty and enga-ging, but his thoughts were only with Laura.

His life without her was a vacuum, without substance, without meaning. He could not be separated from her. He could not have them live on separate continents.

He had to do something.

He decided that he, too, would leave. Emigrate.

He bought a place a few suburbs away from Laura.

That was what the children advised. 'She's not that comfortable with you here. Give her space. Don't be on top of her.'

His apartment overlooked the harbour. During the day, the sea shimmered. At night, lights from the suburbs that stretched from east to west glittered. There was the mystery of the stars and a majestic moon that rode its mystical path.

Steve found himself standing at the window for long moments, in awe of the shifting seas, the brightness of the sun, the brilliance in the dark skies.

He respected what the girls advised. Laura had not received the news of his immigration well. She told them that she did not really want to see him, that she hoped that he would not make a nuisance of himself. She wished that he would get on with his life, make another life, a life that did not include her. She had to be honest, she said. She thought she'd left all that behind.

'Don't worry,' they told her. 'He won't bother you. You'll come across him occasionally – at us, on a Friday night.'

And, 'Try and be gracious about it, Ma. You have your life. Let him try and have his.'

She had the last word. 'As long as that doesn't include me.'

Having wound up his enterprises in South Africa and with consider- able financial backing, Steve set about exploring the business world in Sydney. As he moved from office to office meeting with directors, pro- spective partners or investors, it became apparent to him that he was unfamiliar with the city's business practices. He was also mostly unknown. This was a rude awakening for him. From being a powerful figure in his home city, he was now in unchartered waters. As he moved around the city, he quickly realised that he would need all his wits about him all the time. But there were some good deals to be had, and he did invest in a successful lending business from which he reaped excellent dividends.

His alert mind would not allow him to switch off and he continued to search, even taking a trip to China for what seemed an interesting proposition. Many months were spent on negotiation, but, in the end, to the disappointment of the other directors, he decided to walk away.

He continued to explore opportunities. He was constantly on the lookout for something to do, something to get his teeth into, but eventually, with the passing of the years, he found himself less and less inclined to go through the strain of discussions and digestion of yet another proposition.

He went on long walks. Attended lectures. Learned bridge. Bought a seat in the synagogue. He fetched the grandchildren from school on his allocated days. He found some acquaintances with whom he was comfortable, men with similar interests. He did some travelling, back to South Africa, a trip to the States, an extended holiday to Israel, spending most of his time in Jerusalem, a place that touched his heart and his soul.

He made no women friends, although there were many who, on learning that he was single, invited him over or asked him out. He rejected their overtures. They did not arouse any interest in him.

He was only interested in one woman. His ex-wife Laura.

There were the Shabbats. Friday nights at Carolyn or Arielle.

They came across each other. She was not unfriendly. Civil, that was the word. They got through the evenings as best as possible for the sake of everyone.

'Ma was in a good mood last night,' he remarked to Carolyn as they drove to his grandson's soccer match.

Carolyn stared ahead.

'She's looking lovely, don't you think?' Steve watched his daughter's profile. 'She's glowing.'

The boys jumped out of the back seat of the car and ran up to the field.

She continued to stare through the windshield. 'Yes. She is looking good.' She paused. Then, 'Dad. She's seeing someone.'

'Seeing someone? How do you mean?'

'A man. She met a man. She's been seeing him for the past few weeks.'

'Really?'

'Yes. A very nice man. We met him.'

'She's going out with someone?'

'Yes, Dad. She is. That's why she's happy. They get on really well. They like each other a lot.'

'Laura? Going out with someone?'

'You sound surprised?'

'To be honest, I am surprised. I somehow never thought of Ma with another man.'

'Why not? She's been on her own for a long time. She's an attractive woman. Very good company. Why wouldn't she have someone in her life?'

'I'm not saying that she shouldn't. I just never thought that she would.'

'Well, she is… Lionel, that's his name. He's a solicitor. Retired, or almost retired. I think he works a couple of mornings a week.'

Steve was numb. What he'd just heard was very difficult for him to grasp. Laura with another man.

'We'd better get going, Dad. The game's about to start.' Carolyn walked ahead of him, her slim figure swinging under her woollen jacket.

'OK. I'm coming.' Visibly shaken, a shiver ran through him as he walked to the field, his scarf flapping in the early morning wind.

He saw them in the distance, Laura's dog trotting beside them. He glimpsed them sitting in a café sipping tea.

They were ahead of him in a queue going to a matinee.

He walked into a restaurant and saw them sitting in the window. Hoping they hadn't seen him, he turned round and walked away.

Laura was happy.

She'd found a wonderful companion in Lionel – a kind and gentle man, clever and wise, refined and cultured. They spent their free time together going to films and the theatre, eating in elegant restaurants, walking along the sea, taking long drives into the country.

They travelled to Italy, spent time in France, toured Britain. Wherever they went, he led the way, knowing the places, telling the stories. She found their trips enchanting, and came back excited and wanting to share.

These years were the most painful period of Steve's life. The agony he'd gone through with the loss of Laura was insignificant compared to the realisation that she was now with another man. Seeing them together felt like knives being plunged into his heart.

He was tortured with the thought of them sleeping together. Were they sleeping together? They probably were. Why wouldn't they?

There were days when he did not want to get out of bed, would not shave and walked around in his pyjamas until midday. There were many nights of not sleeping.

His daughters became concerned about him. They asked him what was going on.

He would not say. Excused himself by telling them he was tired. 'A bit under the weather.' Urged them not to worry. Told them it would pass.

They guessed that it was their mother's relationship with Lionel. They phoned every day to see how he was.

Brought him food.

Suggested that he 'see someone' – a doctor, a psychologist. Perhaps go onto antidepressants.

He saw their concern. Realised that he was becoming a burden for them. They don't need this aggravation, he told himself. They've got their families to see to, their husbands, their kids.

He had to pull himself together. To come to terms with it.

Laura was involved with another man. That was her right.

He had to learn to live with it.

Her novel was rejected. Laura was surprised. She believed that it contained some of her best writing.

Her publisher wanted sections redone. He wanted portions edited. He thought it was slow. Lacked the impact of her other books.

She read his comments and went through the manuscript. She rewrote, took out sections, added others.

She read it again and made further changes. She put it aside. Went through it again.

Her publisher was right. It was slow. Boring. The climax didn't work.

Should she rewrite the whole thing? Use the storyline but start again from scratch? She wondered where to start.

She changed it around. Took out a character who seemed redundant. Increased the pace. Sharpened the dialogue. Created more tension.

It did not work.

Perhaps it was the storyline?

She looked through the window. A storm was brewing. In the distance, clouds banked. The sea was flat and oily. A wind howled.

She ruffled through the pages, read a few lines, shrugged and put the manuscript into a drawer.

She dialled a number on her phone and made an appointment to have her nails done.

The phone rang. It was Lionel's son. He was very sorry to let her know that his dad had passed away during the night. It seemed as though he'd died in his sleep. He'd tried to phone him. No one answered. He went to the unit. Lionel was lying in bed. He wasn't breathing.

How had Laura found him in the past few days? Was he himself?

'Yes,' she told him, shocked at the news. 'He seemed OK.' But he did cancel their arrangement yesterday, she said. He was tired. Wanted to take it easy. He hadn't taken her call last night. She assumed that he was resting, or asleep. Said how sad she was to hear the news. How terribly sad.

'He was a lovely man. Really. Such a lovely man.' She had so enjoyed his company. 'I'm very upset. Such a gentleman.'

Was there anything that she could do? For him? For his family? Would he please her know about the funeral?

And the prayers. Where the prayers would be held.

'What happened?'

'They're not sure. Could have been an aneurysm. Or a heart attack.'

'How old was he?' Steve asked.

The girls didn't know.

'In his late seventies,' they estimated. 'Maybe even eighty.'

It was a bright winter day. The sun had taken the chill from the early morning. The air was crisp and still. Fragments of light broke on the sea. Above, the sky was an unbroken palate of washed sea-blue.

Two elderly people sat on a bench opposite anchored boats, an old dog at their feet. He was bald except for a fringe of closely cropped grey hair. Her hair was white, stylishly shaped, curling into the back of her elegant neck.

In front of them, the sea glinted a deep velvet blue and sparkled like diamonds. Children paddled in the shallow waves. A small boy cried.

A girl walked past, as dainty as an oriental doll, her porcelain skin protected by a sunshade.

At the side of the jetty, the ferry offloaded passengers, then waited for others to board.

In the distance, a yacht cut briskly through the waves.

Beside them, the exposed voluptuous roots of a Moreton Bay fig tree formed a sensual sculpture, and above them its wide and spreading branches a lush green canopy.

In the enveloping calm and tranquillity, even the seagulls were quiet.

They talked about their granddaughter's wedding, how beautiful she'd looked, how lovely Carolyn was, how moving the ceremony, how elegant the reception. The meaningful speeches, the handsome accomplished groom, and again, their beautiful and clever granddaughter.

'I've got something for you,' the old man said. From his pocket, he took a piece of wedding cake wrapped in cellophane.

'Oh,' his companion laughed. 'You've still got yours. I ate mine.'

'Yes. I put it under my pillow last night.'

'Did you dream of who you'll marry?' She laughed again.

'I did.' He smiled at her.

'Who was it?' Her eyes teased.

'Need you ask?' His eyes were focused.

'Who was it, Steve?'

'You. It was you.'

'Me? Did you really dream that?'

'Of course. I dreamed that we married and that we had a long and beautiful life together.' He paused. 'Then I woke up and I cried because I know that that's how it should have been. That I ruined everything we had.'

'Steve…'

'Then I dreamed again. I dreamed that I was given a second chance to make it all right. I dreamed that you came back to me and that I took you in my arms and swore by everything holy that I would never hurt you again. That I would love and cherish you every moment of our lives, for the rest of our lives.' He took out a handkerchief and wiped away his tears.

'Steve…'

'You never came back to me, Laura. I know that you couldn't forgive me. I understand that. But I want you to know that, although I don't have you, I continue to love you. I cherish every moment I manage to spend with you. These moments sustain me. They keep me going. You are my life, Laura. You are everything to me.'

She turned to him and patted his large age-spotted hand with hers – white and thin and delicately veined. 'I know, Steve. I know that.'

They looked at each other, faded gold meeting faded blue. She saw his tears in the creases of his eyes.

She took his handkerchief and gently patted the moisture from his face. 'Don't upset yourself,' she said softly.

She slipped her arm through his. 'Come.' She smiled her sweet smile. 'Let's go and have some nice hot tea. I'm absolutely dying for a cup.'